REAWAKENING

CHASE MCPHERSON

Other works by the author:
He's Got Ball(s): Battling Testicular Cancer as a Couple (with Tyler McPherson)

(as Chase Erwin)
The Memoirs of Abel Mondragon:
Vol. 1 - Captivity
Vol. 2 - Echoes of Demons
Vol. 3 - The Great Divide

Cover art by kai Starlight - www.ukiyocomic.com/kai

For Tyler, my warrior.

FOREWORD

A little more than ten years ago, under my given name of Chase Erwin, I began work on a book series called Bloodbound. It was created in part because of my desire to be a self-published author, in part as a type of therapy.

Some aspects of the story were a thinly-veiled attempt for me to reconcile the aftermath of an abusive relationship. In the intervening years I had begun a much more stable relationship, which has since solidified into a devoted marriage – but the self-image issues, the doubt, the flashbacks and memories lingered. Professional therapy, as it so often does, helped. But I still needed an outlet.

I designed the main characters in the image of myself and my new partner, now husband. I put aspects of our real lives in those characters; even some things we have said to one another during our courtship and first years as a couple wound up in the three books I wrote in the initial Bloodbound series.

Having them be vampires was a product of the era. Twilight and True Blood were all the rage on the screens. Throughout their history, however, vampires have been figures of intrigue, danger, and a mixture of emotions. Making them agents of an underworld spy agency was the twist I decided was missing, at least in my estimation – a heroic role.

I wanted a world where vampirism, at least in the role of this agency, was not looked upon with derision or vitriol. This is also why the characters' sexuality is barely discussed - derive your own theories of allegory and real-world connections as you will.

What you're about to read is a reboot, if you will; a reintroduction of the Bloodbound concept, with some key changes to the story. The Hunter character's abusive boyfriend storyline has been withdrawn - it served its purpose when I wrote the first novel. I may revisit the topic if this series picks up steam.

Hunter's path towards a relationship with his partner, now renamed Kai, and to his new career as an espionage agent, will thus change in tack, one that I hope won't be as jarring for the reader as in the original series. No longer will Hunter be the "damsel in distress" starting out. This should put our two protagonists on more of an equal footing in some respects.

I also hope that with the passage of time, I have become a more thoughtful and creative writer. I still have a passion and fondness for the story I was telling, and I sincerely hope you will enjoy this new take on the ideas I had and follow me for the journey.

Yours,

Chase McPherson

FIRST ORDER OF BUSINESS

From what seemed an ages-long purgatorial dream, his vision – or his lack thereof – seemed to quickly transpose into a frame of blinding white light. He quickly tried to analyze his senses. Was there any sound, any shape, perhaps any smell or taste that could make him discover where he was?

Traces of sound, or at least his perception of sound, began to reach his brain. To his left, a repetitive vibration; to the right, the faintest of whistles.

He began to feel various aches and strains to his muscles, including a nagging burning sensation around his middle. He tried to look down to examine his body, but all he saw was the white screen of nothingness.

The sounds began to increase in volume. The guttural vibrations on his left had a distinct rhythm, going up slightly in pitch, then down. Still he couldn't quite place the sound to its proper source. The whistling on his right, however, had transformed into more of a wind. Though he could feel no breeze against his face, he was sure he was hearing a ferocious gale.

He licked his lips in an attempt to gauge any tastes to assist him in his quest to determine his environment. There was no earthen sensation to tell him if he was indoors or out; there was a faint hint of iron on his taste buds, or something metallic... something almost *antique* in a way, as if he'd held a copper coin under his tongue momentarily.

The vibration to his left deepened and intensified yet again, and he became certain this was the sound of some type of wild animal, perhaps giving a warning growl. Panicked, he whirled to the left.

Or he *thought* he had done; there was no physical confirmation he had made any move at all. Only the borderless, white vista in front of him, the sounds of a hungry beast to his left, a storm of unknown proportions whirling to his right.

Where am I?

He strained to remember the last few moments before he apparently lost consciousness... but all he came up with was the realization that he couldn't even remember his name.

Who *am I?*

He suddenly felt a short, hot breath against his left ear. It was most certainly an animal now, the pulsating, vibrating noise taking up almost all his attention. He could still hear wind, but still felt no wind.

The burning sensation against his waistline grew stronger, radiating up his arms and over his shoulders.

He blinked and, for the first time, began to see shadow and the faintest detail of depth. He was indoors. He was laying down, face pointed upward.

The sound of a door unlatching caused him to gasp, and with the sharp intake of air, the white light gave way to a brief snap of black. Blinking again, color and sharpness readjusted themselves in his vision.

He craned his neck to the left. Curled on the pillow next to his was indeed an animal. A cat. A young calico, tufts of gray, brown, white, gold and black dotted about its body, and an unusually thick and bushy tail. Its olive-colored eyes were staring at him, and it was purring. He understood immediately that was the noise he was hearing – an intensely sedate housecat.

The brief moment of joy in decoding that small mystery was replaced by the reminder that he was in a strange room with a door that had just opened, and now closed shut – which meant someone had to have just opened and closed it.

"Wh-who's there," he asked, his voice raspy and dry. He rubbed his eyes.

"Ah, he awakens." The voice was instantly comforting to him, much to his confusion. Though he still couldn't see perfectly, his hearing and smell were working aces. There was a man at the door, taking off what sounded like a thick woolen jacket; the man was also setting aside what sounded like a parcel or maybe a satchel of gear.

It smelled faintly of rain; and it was at this moment a chill met with his skin. He surmised that wherever he was, he was in the middle of a bad snowstorm, now realizing the whistling and howling noise to his right was a hefty wind trying to sneak in between the small gaps of wooden cabin walls.

Heavy leather boots met against creaky floorboards as the man approached his bedside, leaned forward, and switched off the white noise machine. "How do you feel?"

Head still swimming, senses still fine-tuning, he blinked. "Confused." He was not in a cabin after all. The man wasn't wearing a woolen jacket. He had black jeans and a black sweater. There had been no blizzard raging outside.

There wasn't any way to tell what kind of weather there actually was; a long picture window opposite the bed was perfectly sealed by a metallic shutter.

The man nodded, gently sitting on the corner of the bed. The man was young, with almost boyish features: Dark brunette hair, a little ruffled, and soft blue eyes. "Do you remember who you are yet?"

Common sense should have told him this question was not normal, something of a red flag to a normal person undergoing this strange scenario. He could only shake his head.

There was a small understanding smile on the man's face. He slowly pointed to his lips and said with an exaggerated whisper, "Hunter."

Hunter Reeves.

There it was, plain as day. How could he forget his own damn name? *What was going on?*

He took in a sharp breath, and as he exhaled he remembered. "K... Kai?"

Kai looked relieved as Hunter said his name. "That's right."

A cat's paw pressed into Hunter's leg, its claws pricking his skin gently. It caused his muscles to twitch, and a sharp pain from his side made him double over. Startled, the cat dashed away.

"Oh, careful..." Kai said, reaching out for Hunter's shoulder. Hunter was not sure if that gentle scolding was for him or for the cat.

"What happened?" Hunter said. "What's... what's going on?"

A concerned look fell over Kai's face.

"You were... Someone attacked you."

"Who?"

Kai shook his head. "That's not important right now. But they hurt you pretty badly..."

As Kai explained, Hunter looked down and saw that he was bare-chested, except for a large amount of bandaging around his middle. There was more padding around the right side, and there was a dark circle of dried blood.

"...and you're not fully healed yet. You'll need at least one more feeding before the night's over."

Still not putting all the pieces together, Hunter looked at Kai with a puzzled look on his face.

"You were near death, Hunter..." Kai looked ashen and pale as he gathered the words. "I had to turn you."

Turn me?

"I didn't have a choice. I simply could not bear to watch you die. Please forgive me..."

The dizziness began to return as Kai's words sank in and the puzzle pieces began to lock in place.

"Oh."

"...Yeah."

There was an awkward silence as the two men looked into each other's eyes.

"That's it?" After a few moments, Kai broke the silence. "'Oh?' Aren't you upset or angry?"

Sitting upright in bed, Hunter crossed his legs together, clasping the tips of his toes within his hands. He ignored the searing hot sting of atrophied muscles being stretched far beyond their tolerance. "How long have I been...?"

"About a week." Kai fiddled nervously with his fingers as he spoke. "It would have been quicker but, like I said, you were *this close* from dying. You needed a lot of blood just to get back to..." He trailed off before saying the word *normal*.

The cat hopped back on the bed and went directly to Hunter's lap, purring happily. The warmth and comfort spread quickly through his body, and he relaxed back into the pillows.

"Annabelle's been keeping you company the whole time," Kai grinned softly. "She seemed to know when you needed the company."

Hunter scratched behind Annabelle's ears, causing her tail to perk in the air. He sighed.

"So what happens now?"

Kai lifted himself up and he crossed the bedroom to his black backpack. He pulled out a clipboard and a canteen, bringing them both back to the bed. Sitting next to Hunter, he gave him the canteen while he produced a pen from the clipboard.

"We don't have much choice. We have to get you registered. And then we'll have to move you out of General Agency and into V-Division. I can't very well be caught harboring an undocumented vampire in my own ward."

Vampire. The word barely made any sense to Hunter. He knew what a vampire was. He had been around them for so long already, but to actually... *be* one? Shouldn't it feel different? Shouldn't he be in mourning for his mortal life?

"Drink," Kai prodded softly, gesturing to the canteen. "It doesn't stay body temperature forever you know."

Hunter unscrewed the top of the bottle and looked inside. It was filled to the top with thick, dark red blood. He felt nauseous just seeing it.

But he also felt ravenously hungry. He lifted the canteen to his lips and titled it back.

Kai clicked the top of his pen.

"It is my official duty to welcome you to the V-Division of Ward 12, new agent Hunter. Let's begin your onboarding."

2

OPERATING PROCEDURE

Eight months earlier

Kai meticulously scrubbed the rocks glasses, holding each one to the dim light, examining for water spots and putting those he found unsatisfactory back into the dishwasher. If a job is to be done at all, it is to be done right. Even if it was just to keep up appearances.

There were only two patrons at the bar, one at either side. On his left was an attractive but forlorn-looking young man with sandy, ruffled hair. All he'd ordered since Kai's shift began were two ginger ales; the kid just stared into the glass until he noticed the ice had melted, then ordered a new one. To Kai's right, his target - one Edward Messinger. The dossier didn't fudge Messinger's description: a little stout, late 30s, greasy, slicked-back hair and an overall swarthy disposition. He was able to hold his own when it came to the drinks. Hard and fast; in 30 minutes he'd consumed two screwdrivers and two glasses of Castlemaine draught lager without looking ill from the combination.

The music playing in the speakers faded out as the DJ mounted his station and began loading his turntables. A steady stream of clubbers seemed to come out from the black-painted woodwork and within sixty seconds the dance floor was filled, as were the other seats at the bar.

Kai, ever the dutiful bartender, filled orders without stop for 15 minutes. When the first rush wore off, he washed his hands and splashed his face at the prep sink. Patting his face dry, he looked nonchalantly into the mirror. Behind him, he noted three couples of men at the center of the bar - each focused on nothing but the person they were flirting or necking with. On one end, the ginger ale customer; ice melted, swizzle stick with speared cherry at the end anchoring the bottom of the glass. And at the other, Messinger, swiping at his phone screen and half off his stool.

Kai pulled his left wrist to his face as if to examine a cuff or to wipe his brow. "Subject preparing to move," he muttered. Grabbing a glass and the soda gun, he pushed the ginger ale button and looked into the mirror. The DJ cupped one headphone over an ear and pumped his free thumb in the air three times in sync with the beat. *There's my confirmation*, Kai thought. *Mugan has a lock on him.*

In one smooth motion, Kai whirled towards the ginger ale customer, pushed the untouched glass to the side and nudged the new one into position. "I'm not one for cliches," he said, pulling a bottle of whiskey from the top shelf of his workstation, "but if there's anyone in need of a chat with the bartender, it's you."

Thumbing the nozzle off the bottle, Kai poured a shot into the ginger ale and another into a clean glass for himself. Getting no reply, he clinked his glass against the customer's.

Sad Boy blinked a few times, suddenly aware he was being spoken to. He looked at the fresh drink. "Oh, um, no thank you," he whispered. He sounded near tears. "I really should be heading out. How much is that...?"

"Nothing until you drink it," Kai said, slinging the bar towel over his shoulder. "Which you will. Orders from the friendly neighborhood bartender."

The faintest of grins appeared in the corner of the young man's mouth. He took the cocktail and raised it in salutation to the barkeep before taking a swig. Kai tossed his shot back, gave the kid a full-mouthed grin, and turned back to the prep sink. Kai covertly spat the liquor back into the glass and emptied it down the spout. *Fuck,* he thought wistfully. *If there's anything I miss about mortal life it's the ability to knock back the occasional drink.*

The electronic ding of a synthesized bell in his ear brought Kai back to attention. With the growing noise of the bar, the communications team had added a signal that would ring when someone pressed their talk button.

"He's leaving out the front door." Mugan's voice came into Kai's earpiece a second later. "Hayes says the deal is gonna go down in the alley behind the club and the dude's waiting for Messinger to round the corner."

"Copy that," Kai replied into his wrist mic. Turning to face the patrons at the bar, he put on a smile and said, "Sorry folks, I'm short-staffed and I gotta do some quick housekeeping. Bar service is gonna stop for now - just gimme ten minutes!"

There were some sighs of protest but a general sense of acceptance from the group at the bar. Kai noticed the depressed looking guy down the rest of his drink and slide some cash under the glass. He then hopped off the barstool and made a beeline for the restroom.

Hope he gets through whatever's bugging him, Kai thought, before immediately chiding himself. What does it matter? What business of it was his? The kid's not his focus right now - it's capturing and interrogating Messinger... and possibly eliminating him if his role is as crucial as their intelligence had led them to believe.

The men's room door was right next to the swinging door leading to the prep kitchen. As Kai swung past it, he heard a patron loudly complain, "Damn it! This door's always locked when I gotta go so bad..."

Kai swiftly made his way to the back door. There was a garbage bag by the employee exit, waiting. It was filled only with shredded paper, made specifically to give him an excuse for being in the alley. He slowly, deliberately pressed down on the handle to prevent the latch making any unneeded noise.

An L-shaped cinder-brick wall guarded the outside of the door to prevent him being seen until he needed to be. The dumpster was just on the other side of the wall. There was a hole in the wall, large enough for one to put an eye against to see what was going down in the alley. But Kai only needed to concentrate, and allow his ears to pick up any noise going on as Messinger met his man.

"You got the drive?" Messinger asked.

"You... you got the money?" The voice was shaky, obviously nervous. "$500, you said."

"I know I said," Messinger said, aggravated. He reached into the inner pocket of his jacket.

Ding! "Be advised," a female voice whispered through Kai's earpiece. "We detect an unknown subject in the men's room. There's a visual from the window directly above where the deal's going down. Mugan, can you confirm?"

Ding! "Affirmative," Mugan said. "One guy went in a few moments ago."

Kai pressed his talk button. "Don't worry about him, I don't think he's connected to this. Is the exchange done?"

He didn't need to wait for an answer. Messinger spoke. "This better be worth the five hundred," he said. "Otherwise, you'll have hell to pay."

There was a nervous laugh from the man offering the thumb drive. "Of course it is," he said. "It's just what you asked for."

"We'll see about that." Kai could hear a ruffling sound, probably Messinger's inner pockets again.

"I told you, I worked at InnerCore for three months!" The unknown guy was getting more nervous. The pitch in his voice was getting higher. "I was able to hack into their mainframe, no sweat."

"Doesn't mean that's what you're giving me."

Ding!

"He's pulling out a palmtop computer..." the female voice started, before Kai heard the faintest squeaking noise. Where was that coming from?

"... be advised, the men's room window is opening!"

"I'm telling you, man," the high-pitched man's voice got more strained. "Names, addresses, bank account info, everything you wanted. 1,500 files."

"I only see one in the directory." Messinger's voice was getting a harder edge.

"Hayes," Kai hissed, "tell me what you're seeing."

He waited for the earpiece signal for a few precious seconds but didn't hear it. "Hayes!"

"It's a zip file... It-it's..."

A small clicking noise told Kai the palmtop computer was hastily closed.

"Encrypted." Messinger chuckled. "You stupid kid, you were gonna shake me down to unlock the file, weren't you?"

Ding! "Kai, the bathroom guy, he's" –

A large crashing noise interrupted the transmission.

Dropping the garbage bag, Kai whirled around the cinder block wall. He had mere seconds to act.

His rapid senses showed him how badly the situation would deteriorate: Shocked by the sudden noise, Messinger whipped out a pistol from his pants pocket, aiming it at the club's mens' room window, which had just fallen out and shattered in the alleyway. Doing so, Messinger dropped his small computer, letting it crash to the ground.

As Kai flew into Messinger, knocking him down, Messinger pulled the trigger of the gun, the bullet firing into the open window. There was a cry of– surprise? Injury?– coming from the restroom.

Meanwhile, the hacker, the guy offering the thumb drive for cash, hastily grabbed for the computer, yanking the device out and bolting down the alley towards the street.

A blur–a black-cloaked figure Kai knew to be Hayes–swept into the alley, yanking the hacker off the ground.

Messinger still had an iron-tight grip on his weapon. But it was no match for Kai's strength. Kai applied enough force with his left hand to put Messinger's wrist bone to the brink of cracking. He used his free hand to cover Messinger's mouth, muffling his yell of pain. The gun dropped to the ground.

A tall and slender figure came jogging down the alleyway – Mugan, Kai was able to tell right away. "Whatcha got?"

Kai blew an errant strand of hair out of his eyes as he released his hands from Messinger's person. The man writhed and moaned on the ground.

"Things kinda fell apart," Kai said. "I've gotta check on the guy in the bathroom."

Mugan nodded. "What are your orders?"

Kai looked at Messinger again. "Take his computer and bring it to Analysis.

"As for him," he added, growling softly, "isolate. Interrogate. And terminate."

"Yes, boss," Mugan said. With the same swiftness and blur as Hayes, Mugan swept the computer's remains from the ground and whisked Messinger skyward.

Kai rushed to where the bathroom window shattered. With a simple push, he leapt, grabbing onto the top of the club building and swinging his legs into the restroom. Dismounting, he swung easily into the room, landing on the closed toilet seat.

Seated in the corner of the room, shivering and obviously frightened, was his ginger ale customer.

"W... wh... what the fuck did I just see?" His eyes were as wide as saucers.

Kai stood on the toilet, cautiously choosing his words.

"Probably... more than you should have," he admitted. He stepped down from the commode, towards the corner of the room.

His customer's eyes began to water as he advanced.

"Please," the kid begged, "d-don't hurt me..."

"I won't..." Kai began.

The ginger ale customer began to quake even harder as he watched Kai's eye color transform from a soft, everyday blue into a bright, emerald green, with a glow that could easily be seen in the dark bathroom.

"...as long as you are totally honest with me," Kai continued. "And I can be as honest as I can with you."

3

CONNECTIONS

Kai had been through this procedure thousands of times. When his target's eyes locked with his, the connection was made. He could bend their will to his with a simple suggestion. In terms of his job as Chief Interrogator, it was the easiest way to cut through the bullshit; a simple truth-telling command.

The glow and color change in his eyes was part of the influence vampires had over humans. Green was meant to instill calm; it was easier to keep the subject at his ease through a chromatic signal.

"Tell me your name," Kai said. His voice was soft, steady.

"Hunter. Hunter Reeves."

"Can you tell me why you came to the club tonight?"

Seemingly in a trance, Hunter didn't blink, but continued staring directly into Kai's gaze. "I was depressed. I wanted to drink, but I couldn't bring myself to order anything but ginger ale."

"Why did you open the bathroom window just now?" Kai had to assuage his fears that somehow this kid had been part of what had gone down.

"I recognized a voice outside," Hunter said.

"Whose voice did you hear? The older man?"

"No. The one offering the thumb drive." Hunter continued staring into Kai's eyes.

"How do you know him?"

"He's an old f... former friend," Hunter wavered in his response.

Kai took a pause to figure out what to do; he obviously needed to probe Hunter for more details. It required more interrogation, but a growing pounding on the men's room door threatened to derail his concentration. There was no alternative; they'd have to continue their conversation outside.

"I need you to climb out the window and join me in the alleyway," he said.

As if snapped awake from a dream, Hunter blinked and shook his head. "Screw that!"

The response was not what Kai had expected, not what he was used to. The green light in his eyes quickly died out. But he couldn't let the shock sway the situation. He had to retain control.

"Look," he said, "I'm gonna have to unlock the door at some point, and I don't know about you, but I don't want to explain to whoever comes in as to what two guys were doing locked in the bathroom together."

"It's a gay club," Hunter replied. "There's only so many things they're gonna assume."

Kai pondered the retort. "Fair point," he conceded. "But, look – you may be a material witness to a criminal investigation. I need you to work with me here."

Hunter sighed and nodded.

Kai reached for the communication device on his wrist and pressed a button. "I'm coming out with a potential witness. Be prepared to seal the bathroom window once we're out."

Hunter stepped up to the commode and hoisted himself halfway through the window. He looked towards Kai, who had a hand ready to unlock the door. Nodding, Hunter jumped out.

A mere second later, Kai unlocked the door and took a dive through the window as the patrons behind busted through.

Hunter stood, frozen, in the middle of the alleyway, pointed towards the dead end where the dumpster was hastily shoved.

Had he been looking back at the club wall, he would have briefly seen two hazy figures dash past him, slamming a piece of corrugated steel over the window and bolting it to the wall.

However, against the wall, he saw the DJ who had been inside the club a few minutes earlier, with his head buried into the neck of a man with greasy hair. Purple liquid poured from the man's neck and was trickling down the DJ's fingers.

"The fuck?"

The DJ turned his gaze to look at Hunter. He had fangs. They, and his mouth, were smeared with blood.

Hunter spun on his heels. Kai was looking at him again. His eyes were green and glowing again.

"Please stay calm!"

It didn't work. "What the hell is going" –

Before he finished saying the word "on," Hunter blinked and found himself in a seated position. With a few sharp breaths, Hunter realized he was on the roof of the building housing the club, the nighttime Dallas sky-line surrounding him.

Kai was sitting, cross-legged, in front of him. He was talking into his wrist device again. "Clear the area *now*," he said. "Get the cleanup team to the alley on the double."

Tears began to fill Hunter's eyes. "What... what is...?"

Kai softly held up a hand. "Look. I promised to tell you as much as I can," he said. "But I need you to understand: You may be in danger. So please, answer me honestly. For your own safety."

Hunter gulped for air. "Who are you?"

Kai maintained eye contact. He may not be able to influence this guy, he reasoned, but keeping eye contact with him could go a long way towards gaining his trust. "I'm an investigator," he said. "I was investigating the man you saw in the alley."

"The one who- who- who I just saw..."

"Dead, yes." Kai took a labored pause as he decided what to divulge. "He had already been found guilty of his crime and had been sentenced to death."

Hunter blinked, his head swimming. "Don't you have to be in a courtroom to be sentenced to ... don't you have to be in *prison* to be exec... why was the DJ *biting* him?!"

Kai bit his lip. "I have to make some very quick decisions here." He paused again. "The DJ is... a vampire. As am I."

Hunter's eyes once again bulged with shock. "I'm losing it," he said. "Or my drink was spiked or something. Investigator... vampire..."

"I can tell you more," Kai promised, "but I must finish asking you what I need to ask to continue my investigation. You said you knew the other guy. What is his name?"

"Alex Cavas," Hunter said. "He... W-we used to work at InnerCore together. When he said the company's name, I knew that's who was in the alley."

"You didn't know he'd be there tonight?"

"I hadn't spoken to him in weeks," Hunter said. "Not since I quit the company."

Kai nodded, taking Hunter's words as the truth. In decades of this work, he could easily pinpoint when someone was being deceitful. He offered a soft smile. "I have more to ask you, but I'm sure you want to ask some more."

"You did just admit to being a vampire, right?" Hunter's brow was furrowed, deeply concerned.

"Yes, and before you ask–no, we're not all evil, bloodthirsty monsters. Every species has its good and bad actors. I try to live as good. And if you need proof..." He reached into his left pocket and pulled out a black handkerchief. He held it out to Hunter. "Your hand's been bleeding since you got outside. I think you caught yourself on some broken glass."

Hunter looked at his injured hand. Red coagulated blood surrounded a nasty gash. He wrapped the hanky around it. "Thanks," he said softly. "You FBI? CIA?"

Kai shook his head. "I can't tell you precisely who, but it's not a government body I work for."

"What was that thing you've been doing with your eyes?"

This time it was Kai's brows that furrowed. "One of the things vampires can do is influence humans' behavior. We do that with controlled connections - with eye contact. We can cause a person to experience any range of emotion. The color and brightness of our eyes can help extract the result we want.

"If it helps any, green is meant to keep you calm. Did you feel... calm, at any point?"

"Not really," Hunter admitted. "Why is that?"

Kai wasn't certain of his response. "There are some humans who are impervious to vampiric influence. It's... rare. I've never met one, myself."

"Huh." Hunter licked his lips. They were dry and chapped. He suddenly realized he was on a rooftop on an unusually cold-for-Texas January night. "I feel... really tired, all of a sudden," he said. "Could we possibly continue this tomorrow?"

"Only if you promise me you won't skip town on me," Kai said. "I feel I can trust you. I don't want to track you down if I don't have to."

Hunter nodded. "If you want, we could... meet somewhere?"

They stood up simultaneously.

"You're not... afraid of me?"

"I'm not sure what I am at the moment," Hunter said. "I just took in a lot of shit and I need some time to process it."

"I understand," said Kai. "Yes, let's meet up somewhere tomorrow, around 9 p.m."

"How about at the fountain at Anderson Park?"

Kai cocked his head as if to ask why that particular location.

"I always feel comfortable at fountains," Hunter explained. "I think I could be the most helpful to you if I'm comfortable."

The vampire nodded. "Er... do you want me to take you to ground level or" –

Hunter pointed to the ladder at the far end of the roof from where they stood. "I'd rather get down myself, if you don't mind."

Kai nodded and watched as Hunter swung himself over the ledge and onto the rungs of the ladder. In a few seconds, he was gone.

Moments later, Mugan zoomed past the rooftop and landed gently next to Kai, who had sat back down. "You okay, boss?"

"Yeah." Kai appeared frazzled.

"Sorry about that dude seeing me suckin' on the suspect," Mugan said. He had a smooth, British accent. "Is he gonna be alright?"

"Yes," Kai said. "He'll be fine."

Back at his own apartment complex a few hours later, Hunter sat at the foot of his bed, unable to stop thinking about the unbelievable events he had been subjected to. And despite being in the presence of vampires and witness to some sort of crime, not to mention a man's death... He kept thinking about those eyes. Those deep, green eyes.

As the sun rose a few hours later, Kai sat in a windowless office, his legs propped up on a desk, staring at a soulless, buzzing fluorescent light embedded in the ceiling.

Hunter couldn't pick up on his influence. It was a one in a million chance. And he was open and honest the whole time. He hadn't come across someone - a human - like that in ages.

Not since...

And those eyes. Those soft, kind eyes.

The next night, just before the clock struck nine, Kai took the winding trail along the tree-lined border of Anderson Park. He'd been based out of Dallas for nearly ten years, but he hadn't taken the time to really appreciate the beauty the city had to offer. Buildings were impressive, the lights an interesting distraction, but it was the parks, the zoos, the nature still afforded the residents that he enjoyed most. And with his boosted senses, he appreciated so much more - the scent of the wood from each tree, the sound of leaves as they floated to the ground, the coos and hoots from birds and owls perched high above.

He saw the large concrete fountain as he rounded the bend. The oval fountain was surrounded with park benches. And underneath a path light at one of those benches was Hunter. Kai could see he was wearing a very light sweater and khaki pants. One leg was crossed over the other, a black sneaker tapping the air anxiously.

Kai approached closer, careful not to speed toward him as his body willed him to. "You're here a bit early," he said, with a friendly tone. He sat on the opposite end of the bench. He wanted to ensure Hunter he was not to be considered threatening.

Hunter shrugged. "I want to be reliable to you, I decided. I want to help however I can."

"That's good," Kai said. "So let's look past what must have been a completely" –

"Can you fly?"

Kai nodded.

"Is that what happened to Alex last night?" Hunter's voice carried a pining tone, a degree of genuine worry. "Was he flown away from here? Is he... dead?"

"He was flown by one of my agents to be questioned." Kai's voice was soft and deliberate. "No, he is not dead.

Relief washed over Hunter's face.

"You still care about him."

"I can't stand him anymore, but yes, I do," Hunter admitted. "Our mothers died our first year in college. That's what we bonded over; that's what led us to date.

"He lost his way though," Hunter continued. "He became distant. It was like a wall was built between us that I couldn't climb around. But yeah, he was my first real love. I can't separate from that."

Kai had a sudden desire to put a comforting hand on Hunter's shoulder, but restrained himself. The mere notion caught him by surprise: he'd never behave this way around any other subject involved in an investigation. What was compelling him to do so now?

"So you can fly too," Hunter said.

"Yes. Some of the lore you pick up about vampires is true. Flying is one of them. But no, not as a bat. We can't shift our forms. We just... levitate, and with great speed."

"What's keeping you from just... biting into me and killing me right now?"

Kai frowned slightly. "Well, as I tried explaining last night, some of my kind like to practice self-control. I happen to be one of them. There are also other tools I have at my disposal to take care of any unexpected cravings – cravings, I should add, I am not experiencing. So if that sweater neck is getting obnoxious, you can roll it down." He tried adding a small smirk to lighten the mood.

To his delight, it worked. Hunter blushed before chuckling softly and rolling the sweater neck down.

"I need to talk to you about the thumb drive Alex was trying to sell last night," said Kai. "It's protected by a three-layered encryption. We brought it in last night to examine, but our techs tell us it's also got a self-destruct code that will wipe the drive if we test the passwords too many times."

Hunter seemed to recognize the conundrum Kai was posing. "It's how he got his job at InnerCore, actually," Hunter mused. "It's a rudimentary type of code by today's standards, but it impressed the higher ups to hire him in the IT department last year."

"So you may know how to crack it?"

"At least the first two passwords," Hunter said. "He taught it to me when we were living together and he wanted to protect our personal computers."

"Fantastic," Kai said with energy. "What do we do?"

"Well," Hunter closed his eyes. "He takes the file name he's given the root folder or hard drive and he creates a password based on that file name.

"Pretend you've got a keyboard in front of you," he continued, opening his eyes and looking towards Kai. "Let's say for example that the file name is GRAPE, in all capitals. Usually what he'll do for the first password is select characters two keys to the left of each letter in that name."

Kai imagined the keyboard in his office as Hunter suggested. "So, instead of a G, he'd pick... a D."

"Right," Hunter confirmed. "And for the R, it'd be a W."

"What about the A? There's only one key to its left."

"Then you'd go up to the next row and hit the key furthest to the right," Hunter answered. "And since the A was capitalized, you'd hit the shift key. So on my keyboard, that'd be the vertical line character. And in his method, you skip every non-character key except the delete key. So if the letter were Q, you'd hit delete and move on to the next character.

"And if the character were on the top row and you ran out of keys, you'd start over again at the right-side of the first row of characters. The second password is exactly the same. You start with the capital A but move two keys to the *right*."

Kai pulled out his smartphone and began sending a text message. "I'm telling our tech guys to follow these instructions. I'm certain you're right that this is the method to get those first two encryptions."

"I'm afraid I'm not sure about the third," Hunter said. He rose from the park bench and crossed to the fountain. He sat on the cool cement rim and absently put a hand in the water. "He changed the third one constantly.

And he never told me how I was able to log into my computer without needing it."

"It's a tremendous first step though," Kai said. He smiled at Hunter again, only to again be hit with a pang of guilt. *Guilt over what?* He thought. *Griffin has been gone for so many decades now...*

"Is there something else you'd like to ask about... me, or what's going on here?"

Hunter shook his head slowly. "Probably a lot, but I can't think right now." He took his hand out of the fountain water and shook it.

"For someone who just recently confirmed the existence of vampires, you're taking it in stride," Kai observed.

"I've learned to take shocks as they are -- just things that have happened. No sense in contemplating how big or small the event is. It's real, and there's no changing it. It's just that last night were four or five big shocks in a row - bam, bam, bam." Hunter looked directly into Kai's eyes. He began to speak again, but--

Kai's phone lit up and buzzed. He looked at the screen for a moment, then frowned.

"What happened?"

"They got the first two passwords to work using your instructions. But then the drive ran a program automatically when the second password was accepted. They weren't even prompted to enter the third - it just ran the program... and then fried the drive. It's totally unusable. Damn..."

Hunter turned his head to one side, gazing absently towards the amber light of the path light near them. "I have a thought..."

"Yes?"

"I wonder if Alex still lives in that apartment in Arlington."

Kai's ears pricked up. He rose from the bench and sidled up to Hunter. "Tell me. What are you thinking?"

"I still have a copy of his key," Hunter said.

Kai smirked coyly. His natural investigative instincts told him they maybe hadn't hit a dead end so quickly. "Field trip?"

"Only if you don't mind a rideshare," Hunter said, taking out his phone. "I don't think I have the stomach for a midair vampire flight."

As Hunter turned to order the car, he added under his breath, "at least, not yet."

Kai heard him.

CURRICULUM VITAE

The pair didn't say a word during the nearly 30-minute car ride from Anderson Park to the Fields of Arlington Grange apartment complex. Kai traded pleasantries with their driver to avoid being rude, but Hunter was deep in thought, staring at his phone, which wasn't on. His spare hand was in his right pocket, thumb and forefinger placed on a key he had washed with the jeans hundreds of times, but never bothered to remove.

When the car pulled up to the gate, Hunter jumped out. Kai followed behind. Without missing a beat, Hunter tapped in the gate code and hustled past the wrought iron the moment the gap between the halves was wide enough.

Kai spent a brief moment looking at the complex. Beautiful, seven-floored buildings, with gable-top roofs. Lush greenery on every block. A centralized office with a pool, lights dancing on its surface. A quaint, suburban complex.

He then realized he was quickly losing ground to his companion again. Kai jogged up to Hunter. "Are you alright?"

"I'd rather just get this done," Hunter said. With Kai just a step behind, Hunter paced to the end of the main avenue of the complex before banking to the right. He buzzed down the walkway leading to Building 3. "It's the top floor," he said, without turning to face Kai. He was trying not to let his reddening face or the fact he was near tears show.

A moment later, they were at Apartment 3721. Hunter had the key in the lock, but his fingers were quivering.

"Shall I?" Kai offered. Hunter nodded. "You should probably stay out here anyway. At least until I clear the apartment."

"Clear it?"

"You never know," Kai explained. "Some kook could have his place wired to explode the second an uninvited guest" --

"What do you think he is?" Hunter snapped. "He's not a criminal mastermind! He's just..." his voice trailed. "He's just *not.*"

Kai nodded and made sure Hunter saw his eyes as he spoke. "I didn't mean to suggest that. In this line of work I have seen just about everything so I have learned to prepare myself."

Hunter nodded, trudged to the wall opposite the door, and waited, arms folded.

Kai pushed the key all the way into the lock, turned it, and opened the door cautiously.

And waited.

Silence.

Kai crept inside, then made a swift check, room-to-room. About 30 seconds passed before he stuck his head back into the hallway. "I think we're cool. I may need your help inside, though," he said to Hunter, who took a deep, labored breath, and followed inside.

Snapping the living room light on, Hunter found a familiar, yet strange sight. He remembered the layout of the apartment when he and Alex lived together. While it remained similar, what struck Hunter was how few possessions remained. Bookshelves once filled with manga, biographies, and discs the two enjoyed and shared... gone. Posters that once hung on the walls torn down -- ripped, leaving shreds of paper pinned to the drywall.

"So what was this idea you had?" Kai prompted.

"First, I assume you'll probably need to take his computer in to be examined, right?"

"Yeah."

"'Kay. Well, for starters," he pointed to a white square object mounted above the front door. "I need you to remove that from this room. Maybe toss it in the dumpster behind the building.

"What is it?"

"It's a high-powered magnet. It can erase traditional computer hard drives if they cross its path. That's why there's nothing electronic along that wall."

Fascinated, Kai closed the front door and looked up at the magnet from underneath. "Paranoid much?"

Hunter nodded with a rueful grin. "He was so into LAN parties and had guys over all the time until he started work at InnerCore. Then that stopped and the overbearing security measures took over."

"Is there a stepladder?" Hunter motioned to the utility closet down the hallway, and Kai procured the ladder. He took a small screwdriver from a pouch in his pants pocket and began dismantling the magnet.

Hunter stood in the living area, then walked to the kitchen. He opened the cabinets and the fridge. All bare. He watched Kai unhook the magnet and waited as he left to dispose of it.

"I'm also certain that wasn't the only thumb drive Alex had," Hunter said when Kai returned, as he crossed to the bedroom. "If he was trying to sell it to one person, he would have tried to offer it to others. Probably at the same time."

"Seriously?" Kai seemed incredulous. "That's a rookie move, trying to criss-cross."

"Precisely," Hunter said. "He was desperate, but for what, I don't know."

In the bedroom, steps away from a queen mattress with no linen, was a fake oak computer desk, one hastily assembled from a cheap department store kit. An impressive widescreen monitor sat on its top. A large metallic PC tower sat to its right. Hunter began unhooking cables and cords, then spun the tower around to show Kai the panel. He pointed to a small device, no bigger than a thumbnail, attached to one of the USB ports.

"The computer he built for me has one of those things too," Hunter explained. He pulled out an identical device from his left pocket. "I think that this is why I never needed the third password. This thing might contain a bypass-or the password itself."

"So if someone else tried to access it without that thing," Kai said thoughtfully, "the thumb drive would self-destruct."

Hunter nodded. "It's just a theory, but it's the only thing that would make sense to me."

"It's a good one," Kai reassured him. "And yeah, it might be just as well to try that out on his own PC. But we're forgetting - we don't have that thumb drive anymore. You said there might be others."

"If there are, we'll have to look for them."

They spent about an hour combing through the apartment, checking and re-checking drawers, cabinets. They tried the water heater, the utility room, and even the boxes of baking soda left in the freezer. There was no trace of additional drives.

"Hmm. It was a good thought," Kai said. "But maybe there just aren't any."

"It's not his way, though," Hunter said. "His whole thing was to go hard if he was dedicated to something. He would cut corners, though. To save time or just out of laziness..."

Hunter stopped. He thought. He smiled. He went back to the bedroom. Kai followed.

Hunter got on his knees and went underneath the desk. "Aha!" There was the sound of something being ripped, and seconds later, Hunter sat upright, holding a long piece of Scotch tape with two USB drives stuck to it.

Kai looked at it in disbelief. "You're kidding," he said. "No box below the floorboards? No false-bottom can of soda - just taped under the desk?"

"Told you," Hunter said, "laziness."

"For him, maybe, but you..." Kai crossed the bedroom and sat down in front of Hunter. "You're... incredible."

Hunter balked, causing Kai to backtrack. "In-in this. Investigating. You know Alex's M.O. so well: You knew about the magnet, you knew about there being multiple drives. And you figured out about this other thing plugged into the computer."

"Now wait. That's still a theory," Hunter protested, blushing.

"Even so, it's a great one and I bet it has legs," Kai said. "We just have to take it to headquarters and see for ourselves."

"Headquarters?" Hearing it back made Kai cringe a bit. There wasn't any other way, he reasoned. "Yes. Hunter, I know you've had a lot go on in the past 24 hours, and I hate to slam you with some more stuff to process..."

Hunter nodded. "It's okay. I... I trust you."

If he had the need for a heartbeat, this is where it would have skipped -- Kai fought back old memories and carried on with what he was trying to say. "You are proving quite vital to this investigation. "I'm likely to have more need for you while we do this. I'm gonna have to ask you... to work with me."

"Work with you." Hunter's voice was flat. "Not even FBI asks people to just work with them."

"I'm not with the FBI," Kai reminded him. "This is something... off-sides. And deeper, if that makes sense."

Hunter shrugged, as if to say, "How could any of what's been going on make sense?"

"So, we'll take the computer down to headquarters, you'll help us gain access to what we need, and I'll fill you in on what's about to happen."

Hunter pointed to the giant PC. "Won't it be weird lugging that thing into a rideshare into... I'm assuming downtown? At this hour of the night?

Kai whipped out his phone. "We won't be taking a rideshare this time."

A sleek black Town Car was waiting by the time Hunter and Kai, carrying the large computer unit, made it back to the gate. Kai secured it in the trunk, and the pair got into the backseat.

As they drove back into the city, Hunter had come up with more questions for Kai. "Is the daylight thing true?"

"Sadly," Kai nodded. "Sometimes it's hard to believe I haven't seen a natural sunrise or sunset for more than 160 years."

"160!" Hunter gasped.

"That's the other thing that's true," Kai said with a sad smile. "Despite our true age, we'll never look more than the age we were when we... crossed over. I'll always look like I'm in my late 20s."

"Wow..." Hunter was at a loss for more words on the topic. He looked out his window as they entered the heart of downtown Dallas. They passed by an old television transmitter tower, whose red toplights continued blinking to life and fading over and over.

"We're here," Kai said.

"Seriously?" Hunter said in surprise. "I thought this was just an abandoned TV studio."

"To everyone else, it is," Kai explained. "For me, it's my office."

The car turned towards a loading dock at the rear of the building. A large metallic door began to lift, and the car passed through.

"I have to ask you now for your utmost silence on the things you're going to see and hear in this building," Kai said. "I cannot, under *any circumstances*, get wind of you telling somebody about this place.

"And, I'm sorry about how fast things are moving," he added. "I can't say it's going to slow down anytime soon."

"It's okay," Hunter said, unaware his hand was moving towards Kai's. "Like I said... I trust you."

Kai hesitated and reached for Hunter's hand. But just as his fingers were about to clasp around, the car jerked to a sudden halt. "We're here," he said. "Just stay by my side, okay? I'll explain everything as we go."

"I will."

The two men exited the vehicle. Joining Kai's side, they walked at a deliberate pace. Every so often someone would walk by, hand something for Kai to sign, then scuttle away hurriedly.

"This is the headquarters for Ward 12 of a group called The Order," Kai began. "We are what you'd call an underground organization, not beholden to any one government. We are like them in the sense that we investigate certain heinous crimes. We assist them when asked, but by and large we run on our own agendas. The Order's leadership hands down our assignments. We lead our own teams. We report the information we get back through the chain of command, and from there, they determine what punishments, if any, should be handed down.

Trading more files from a few more people, Kai reached an elevator door and pressed the call button for it. A bell rung, the doors opened, and he and Hunter stepped inside.

The car jerked as it started. Hunter could feel from the car's motions that rather than just going down, it was also moving *left*... then *forward*, then *left again.*

"You may ask why we have the authority to levy punishments," Kai continued. "It's simply because the world's governments always seem to have their hands too full to even deal with the things you hear about on the news. World leaders perpetrating war crimes is already enough without more people on the brink of causing international incidents."

The elevator came to a complete stop. Bells rung again and the doors opened onto a vast, warehouse-sized room with two floors. Certain offices were closed off in walls of glass. A large bank of computer monitors spitting out data and video information covered the wall of the second floor. It actually looked to Hunter like he imagined a large city TV newsroom might look. Kai stepped out, followed closely by Hunter, as he continued to speak.

"I'm about to officially ask my supervisor to add you to my team," Kai said. "You will help me on this and any other investigations that come around... if you want.

"But I have to warn you," Kai added. "If you don't -- and if so, I totally understand -- but you would have to expect to be followed and monitored for a great deal of the rest of your life." He stopped in his tracks, and he put both his hands on Hunter's shoulders, causing the human to shiver. "The public can't know about The Order,"Kai said, "and your knowledge just of what you've seen getting to this spot here is valuable to far too many of our enemies."

"Interrogator!" boomed a voice from the far end of the vast office. Kai snapped to attention immediately as a man, portly and balding, but sharply dressed in a black pinstripe suit, made large strides from his rear office towards the pair. "Is this your potential recruit?"

"It is, sir."

As the man reached them, Hunter had to remind himself to breathe. It wasn't that the man himself seemed intimidating, but the severity of the situation warranted extreme silence, so he had been holding his breath.

"Hunter Reeves," Kai began. "This is Chief Winston Calhoun."

With Calhoun about five inches taller than Hunter, the chief did appear to look downward toward him. Calhoun held out his hand, without breaking a smile. Hunter hesitated, which caused a small chuckle from the imposing figure.

"If Interrogator Taylor had instructed you not to speak, you can consider that order relieved," Calhoun said with the smallest of smiles. Hunter just nodded, and offered his hand in greeting.

Kai Taylor, he said, realizing he had never asked for Kai's last name.

"Come," Calhoun said after shaking Hunter's hand. "Get me up to speed."

The chief spun on his heels and headed back to what was clearly his office. Kai followed one pace behind, with Hunter lagging as he gathered more of his wits.

"We recovered the computer belonging to our hacker," Kai reported. "We also have more thumb drives; they're all on their way to the tech team now. We also have reason to believe there was an additional device required to open the thumb drive safely."

"I see," Calhoun said, opening his office door for the two men. "When will we see results?"

"Likely within the hour," said Kai. "And we might not be saying that if it weren't for Hunter here." He offered Hunter a reassuring smile that Hunter appeared to take comfort with.

"I see," Calhoun said again. There was a pause. Eyes darted from person to person. "And this is why you recommend him for agency status?"

"It is," Kai said. His eyes rested on Hunter's once more. "Beyond a sharp, insightful knowledge, he has shown me to be rather capable of handing rapid changes of situational awareness.

"I see."

Man of few words, Hunter guessed. Either that or Calhoun was simply weighing the pros and cons of this new person standing, and starting to sweat, in front of his desk. Calhoun's voice was weathered, somewhat reflective of the man's age, Hunter noticed. It prompted him to ask a question.

"Are you a vampire, too?"

Calhoun seemed surprised, if not by the question itself, then by finally hearing Hunter's voice. "Ah, no," he answered, his expression softening. "The Order only recently, say in the last 70 years or so, began associating itself openly with vampires. Please, sit," he added, gesturing to the chairs before them. The three men sat down.

"The V-Division was created by Calhoun's great-grand-father," Kai explained. "I helped organize it and recruit their first vampire agents."

"Sidwell Calhoun," the chief said, almost wistfully. "I never got to meet him, but his exploits with Taylor here are legendary. I don't know how much you know about Texas legends, but the so-called Railroad Ripper from the early 1900s was captured by the pair of them."

Hunter shook his head.

"Ah," Kai sighed. "It's a story you'll have to hear when you get the chance."

"To get back to the matter at hand," said Calhoun, "how it works is I oversee this ward's operations, which usually involves recruiting new agents. Kai watches over the V, or Vampire, division, and is normally the recruiter for them."

"Since they're all vampires," Kai added. "But you're not, so I felt it was obligatory to have Calhoun sign off on your hiring."

"You would technically be working for Kai, but under my jurisprudence," Calhoun said.

It made no sense to Hunter; he was beginning to fill overwhelmed again. But after such glowing praise from Kai, he felt he had to agree just to keep the pace of the meeting going.

"You'll need to understand," Calhoun said. "Now is your 'don't turn back' moment. I'm sure Kai explained, if you choose not to join us, you will be under surveillance for many years. I want to be upfront about this. You will lose some semblance of privacy for quite a long time. And Kai will have to disavow all knowledge of you from here on out."

Hunter froze. He had honestly been considering refusing the offer when it came down to it -- how could he possibly be working for an underground investigation agency with its own rules of law and order? But the thought of not being with Kai, not learning more about him...

"If you do choose to remain with us," Calhoun continued, "it is not an 'at-will' arrangement. You are with us for the long haul. Until we decide to retire you, or until your death separates you from us, you are dedicated to working for this agency."

This time, it was Kai who froze. He'd heard the warnings before, but suddenly connecting the concept of death with Hunter made him feel particularly sad.

"Your life will be making a permanent set of changes," Calhoun said. "Changes to your social life, your current living situation -- you will essentially stop living like you currently are."

There was a thick silence that hung in the air after Calhoun finished. Hunter thought carefully about his next set of words.

"I believe I understand what's at stake here," Hunter said. "And I think I know the risks involved with my choice. And while you say there will be changes to my life, I would argue there are no changes that could make that life worse than how it's been as of late." The words surprised Kai. He suddenly remembered how sad Hunter had looked at that club just one night ago. He also realized he didn't really know Hunter at all. He just had this sense, a general estimation, of who he was.

"But I was never going to change my life without some provocation," Hunter mused. "This seems like as good a chance as ever. If I'm being offered a position here, I would like to take it."

"Very well." Calhoun planted a palm on his desk, which made Kai and Hunter jump in their seats. "Interrogator, let's get the paperwork started.

"Hunter Reeves - welcome to the secret world of The Order."

5

ORIENTATION

Over the next several weeks, Hunter's life did undergo even more swift changes, just as Kai and Calhoun had warned. The very next day, in fact, at Hunter's apartment, he was awoken by a loud banging at the door.

"Movers!"

What the hell? Hunter groggily looked at his alarm clock. It was just barely 10 a.m. He opened the door to find an entire moving crew waiting outside.

"Movers," repeated the man at his doorstep.

"There's got to be some mistake," Hunter said, stifling a yawn. "I didn't hire any" --

"I'm with The Order," the man whispered. "Calhoun sent me. The name's Addison."

Hunter's eyes widened. "You'd better come in," he said.

"We've been given instructions to gather all your things and have them held until Mr. Calhoun and Mr. Taylor have made new living arrangements for you," Addison said. He was dressed in authentic-looking mover's apparel, complete with those disposable slippers they slip over their shoes.

Hunter put his hands on the top of his hands and sighed. He wanted to protest, but he *had* been told -- *You will essentially stop living like you currently are.*

"Where am I supposed to go in the meantime?"

Addison lifted the brim of his trucker's hat and scratched at his clipboard while he looked it over. "You're to undergo testing at H.Q. until Mr. Taylor arrives to start the evening shift," he read.

Hunter threw up his hands. "Alright then," he said. "Let me just grab a few things to take with me."

"If this first day is any indication, I don't think I'm going to have the strength to be in this place," Hunter mumbled.

He lay outstretched on a black leather sofa next to Kai's desk. Kai was seated at his computer, typing rapidly.

"I'm sure it wasn't that bad."

"It was like three physicals, two gym tests, and that-that thing, you know, where you pedal that thing in the water?"

"A catamaran?"

"Yeah, that -- all put together. And all that was before I took the SAT."

Kai laughed. "We call that the GAT. Generalized Aptitude Test."

"I called it a pain in the ass," Hunter grumbled.

"My, you're grumpy," Kai said. He stood up from his chair and knelt beside Hunter. He took one of his hands. "You're through the worst of it; those won't be happening again."

"I know," Hunter sighed, "and I'm sorry. I didn't get much sleep before running that gauntlet of tests. And I just didn't expect all my stuff to be packed up this fast."

"We have to move quickly," Kai said, "it's just how we have to roll."

Hunter looked at Kai's hand holding his. Kai noticed and pulled his hand back swiftly. "I-I'm sorry."

"You don't have to be," Hunter mumbled.

"Hm?"

"I said, you don't have to be." Hunter looked at him. "I get it, you feel something. I do too. But I've been burned so many times acting so fast. But having to pack up my life is happening so fast - I'm so confused by everything!"

Kai nodded. "I get it. That's why I had an idea, even though it might complicate things more. We both agree, we feel *something* together. But we need time to explore it. So what if... what if we moved you to my place?"

Hunter blinked. "Your place? Like... roommates?"

"Yeah. I have a spare room; you're welcome to it." Kai put his hands in his pockets. He looked to Hunter almost bashful as he picked his words. "Maybe we start just as friends and roommates. If things don't work out, we can still set you up at one of the complexes most of the agents use. And if things *do* work out, then..." He trailed off.

Hunter gave a soft smile. "Do you have a soaking tub?"

"This is *fantastic,*" Hunter moaned. The jets were pointed right at his sorest muscles, causing an already bountiful amount of suds to grow even further.

"I like deep baths too," Kai said from the doorway. "But you might have at least waited for the moving crew to finish hauling everything in."

"Don't mind us, Mr. Taylor," Addison said from the far room. He was carrying in a mattress with a partner. "Remember, we've seen worse cleaning up those crime scenes!"

"What was that?" asked Hunter.

"Never mind," sighed Kai. "Oh, Hunter, you might like this..."

He tapped a button on a control panel by the bathroom door. The bright white lights faded out, and a set of blue lights illuminated the room from under the surface of the bathwater.

"Holy crap," breathed Hunter. Kai grinned and wordlessly left the room.

Later, once the movers had left and Hunter had changed into a pair of pajama pants and an old Coheed & Cambria tour T-shirt he'd packed that morning, he and Kai sat at the same side of Kai's black dining table.

"This place is so ultra-modern," observed Hunter. "Nothing like a place I'd expect a vampire to live."

Kai shrugged. "To each his own, I suppose. I like living a bit of luxury; it makes up for all those years I had to sleep in hovels or forests or deserts."

"What?"

Kai sighed. "So, it was 1862. I had run off from my family farm in North Carolina. I was intent on joining the war."

"1862... *the Civil War?!*" Hunter tried, and failed, to keep his mouth from dropping open.

"'Civil' War... there's a misnomer," Kai said bitterly. "Anyway, I had no trouble enlisting, I was of age. And there was a battleship off the coast of Cape Hatteras that was willing to take me on. I was a crew member for precisely two days."

"What happened?"

"That ship happened to be the U.S.S. Monitor," Kai explained. "It was weakened in previous battles. But it turned out to be a stormy night and rough waters that did her in. It sank, and I was one of the few to make it off that ship alive.

"But whereas the other survivors were met by a rescue ship, I had floated out away from them. And I'm sure I would have been lost with about 16 other crewmen, if it hadn't been for a rogue vampire who had an eagle-eyed view of the disaster unfolding."

Hunter picked up his legs and crossed them in his seat. He was completely engrossed in the story.

"He just plucked me out of the water and flew me to his house back on shore. I never even had a chance to see where I had been taken or to even thank him for pulling me away from the wreck... before he plunged his fangs into me.

"I never even knew his name. The turning process takes several days, you see. And in that time, someone had alerted the townspeople that a vampire was in their midst. By the time I was waking up from the change, the vampire had already been staked, and the house was in flames.

"God..." Hunter whispered.

"A good vampire is supposed to teach his progeny all about his new life, his new abilities," Kai said. He was staring at the wall in front of him, transfixed on a framed photo of a forest. "I had to learn by instinct. I flew to the

nearest thing I could reach - a bank of trees further in-
land. I lived there, like an animal, for... I don't know, at
least three months. I fed on wildlife, I slept underground.

"If you're not taught soon within that window of time,
you stay feral," Kai continued. "It was sheer luck there
had been a small tribe of traveling vampires making their
way through that forest. They sensed my presence; they
did what they could to teach me how to maintain some
amount of my humanity.

"I stayed with them for nearly a year," he said, "before
I knew I needed to break out on my own, see where I
could make a living. By that point I was here in Texas."

"That sounds so much like my life," Hunter said.

Kai's eyebrows arched. "How so?"

"Well, not *so* much like my life," Hunter corrected. "I
lived in rural Nebraska all through high school. I'd been
teased for being gay starting in grade school - I didn't
even know what it meant until sixth grade!

"But anyway, when I graduated I wanted to get as far
away from there as I could. I went to the first college that
accepted me. That was here in Dallas. But even though I
was a bright kid, the thing I never learned growing up
was how to have friends. I tried, but I was so overenthu-
siastic, so starved for companionship, I drove a lot of
people away.

"That's when I was diagnosed as depressed," Hunter
continued. "I rarely went to class, I was convinced the
people laughing as I passed them by were laughing at
me, because it was all I was used to."

Kai nodded as he took in Hunter's story.

"Eventually I met Alex, and I found a kindred spirit in him," Hunter said. "Like I told you, our moms died while we were in school - within a month of each other, actually. We really leaned on each other then. And I was the one who pressed to make it through as a couple. Alex didn't want to, at first, but at some point he decided it wasn't worth waiting to see if someone else would ever have the feelings I was developing for him. And so we decided to make a go of it. That's when we both got hired at InnerCore, and know you know the rest of the story."

Kai looked at Hunter. He knew he'd have to tell him this eventually. "The only one I ever loved before was named Griffin. I killed him. I killed my only lover."

Hunter opened his mouth to speak, but Kai continued, the words forcing their way out. "I didn't mean to! He was a human farmer. It was the 1960s. We were all alone in the world. He asked me to turn him - I didn't want to, at first! But he pleaded with me. I loved him so much and I didn't want to think about living without him. I-I thought I was doing it right. I brought him to the brink... the brink of... d-death... and I drank too much. You're supposed to stop right at the brink, you see, then give him one mouthful of your own blood to start the process. But... I took one sip too much.

"I had promised myself I would never kill if it wasn't tied to the job, or for a life-or-death matter. I told myself I was not a monster. But I killed him. He just... laid there, in my bed. His eyes were still open. I opened my wrist and gave him my blood... and it just poured right back out of his mouth, and into the sheets... onto the floor."

Kai hid his face in his palms, sobbing. Hunter raced to the kitchen and grabbed some paper towels. He folded one up several times over and motioned for Kai to move his hands. When he did, Hunter saw vampire tears. They were almost identical to those of humans: translucent, but tinged with red. He dabbed at Kai's cheeks with the paper towel.

"It was an accident," Hunter said softly. "It's perfectly understandable. You didn't know how to control yourself, obviously. I'm sure he wouldn't have wanted you to carry that around all this time.

Kai sniffed. "I haven't allowed myself to have feelings for any human else since then," he said. His voice was a quavering whisper. "And I'm scared that I have them for you. They're so strong, Hunter. I can't ask you to turn for me, and I don't know if I can commit to someone I know is going to grow old and die. I just... don't know."

Hunter dabbed more at Kai's face. "First of all, let me say how flattered I am you would even consider me to be your roommate, let alone a companion, a partner, a co-worker, *whatever*," he said. "I don't trust myself, either - at least in terms of relationships. Not after Alex. "All we have right now is time. That could be a blessing or a curse, I don't know which. But let's just promise ourselves this. We trust our instincts, no matter how they've betrayed us in the past. Okay? Let's not worry about what may happen down the line, and focus on what's going on in the moment."

A sharp growl of air bubbles coming from Hunter's stomach interrupted that particular moment. Both men looked at each other and laughed.

"That's right, I didn't actually eat anything today," Hunter mused.

"We can order anything you like," Kai said, wiping his eyes dry. "We can have it delivered to our security guys down the road; they'll bring it up to us."

"What about you?" Hunter's curiosity peaked again. "What do you normally... do about that?"

Kai gestured to the refrigerator. "Whole thing's stocked. There are hospitals who are in The Order's network that will supply us as needed," he explained. "If you wouldn't mind... could you pop a container in the microwave for me? 48 seconds gets it to prime temperature."

Hunter was intrigued by what this would look like. "Sure," he said. He opened the door to the fridge. 150 plastic containers, all filled with bright red blood, jiggled when the door hit Hunter's hand.

Grotesque, he thought to himself, but interesting, nonetheless. He grabbed a random bottle from the door, twisted off the cap, and set it in the microwave. He set the timer and watched the turntable spin the bottle slowly in a counter-clockwise motion.

"May I... could I at least hug you?" Kai asked.

Hunter nodded. "I know I would like it."

Kai sat up from the able, wiped his eyes again, and stepped into the kitchen. He wrapped his arms around Hunter and pulled him into a hug that lasted until the microwave beeped.

"Blood's done," Hunter said with a wry smile. Kai laughed. Hunter opened the door and took out the bottle. Kai opened the nearby drawer and pulled out a stainless steel straw, plopping it in the bottle. He took several gingerly sips from it. "Perfect," he said.

Hunter just stood there and watched Kai suck down the blood from the bottle. It reminded him a lot of watching someone drink V8 juice.

"Do you ever tire of the taste," he asked.

"Sometimes," Kai admitted. "But our guys at the lab? Some of them have backgrounds in food additives. They can make it smell or taste like practically anything I want."

"Amazing," Hunter whistled.

"You wanna get that food order placed now?" Kai went back to the dining room table and turned on his tablet.

Hunter nodded and joined him at the table. As they waited for the order to be delivered to security, Hunter put his arms around Kai's waist.

"This feels... right," he said. "Know what I mean?"

"I do," Kai nodded.

"And I really, truly don't want you to think too much about my dying, or turning me, that kinda thing," Hunter added. "It's too soon to be having those kinds of conversations."

"I promise I won't," Kai said, knowing it might be difficult at first to try.

"Besides," Hunter said, "if it ever comes to it, I know you'd do it right this time around. I trust you."

With each passing day, Hunter learned more about his job at The Order. As a Researcher, he was tasked with looking up information on many varied cases. Biographies, histories, technical schematics, and delivering them to various other departments. But for at least two hours every day, he would meet with Kai and Calhoun to give them more information about his life before joining the order - and in particular, his history with Alex and the places they used to spend time together.

"We would hang out at least three times a week at Electric Six," Hunter said at their most recent meeting, referencing the club where the sting had been set up. "That's probably why he chose it as a meetup point, come to think of it. He'd know every exit, every nuance of that building before he'd consider something like that."

Kai turned on a TV screen on Calhoun's wall. "When we finally confirmed that dongle plugged into Alex's PC was necessary to prevent his encrypted USB drive from self-destructing, we confirmed that the data he was selling was a list of people who had worked at InnerCore." He used a remote control to scan through a series of slides that included employee photo identification and contact information for each person.

"Do you see any patterns in this, Hunter?"

Hunter squinted as he watched each slide pass by. "Not really," he said. "Many of them are blond-haired and blue-eyed." He paused. "Wait, you don't think this is some sort of Nazism, Aryan race bullshit, do you?"

"Not for a second," Calhoun said flatly. Hunter felt a twinge of embarrassment for even suggesting it.

Kai continued flipping through slides.

"Here's something else," Kai said.

"Employee status, resigned," Hunter read, following Kai's finger across the screen. "Separation date, December 18th... 'DRS status, selected?' What does that mean?"

"That's what we're trying to figure out," Calhoun said.

"At least one pattern here is that everyone listed in this file was either fired or resigned," Kai said. He flicked through a few more slides to prove his point. "No retirees. None of the executives."

"We obtained employee files for those who led the company or who retired after 15-plus years of service," Calhoun said. "None of them have a DRS status at all."

"Was there anything that seemed weird about the onboarding process when you and Alex got hired?" Kai rubbed his chin as he asked.

"Let's see," Hunter thought. "We had the usual tax forms to fill out, we sat through about a whole day's worth of company policy and anti-sexual harassment videos, like everywhere else I've ever worked... Wait. The vaccinations..."

Calhoun nodded. "It's a biotech firm. InnerCore may have made some vaccinations compulsory as a condition of employment."

Kai turned back to the screen and flipped through some slides. "Quite a few of these termination dates were just two days after their start date," he noted. "Did you and Alex get the vaccinations?"

Hunter nodded. "They were given on our second day," he said with a raised eyebrow. "They had told us they were working with potentially dangerous viruses and these were a layer of protection should there be a breakout of some sort."

Calhoun rubbed the bald spot on his head. "And they didn't say what, specifically."

"No."

"I have a copy of the spreadsheet here," Calhoun said. "Many of these who were dismissed after only two days have a DRS status of "ineligible" ... and all of them cite a termination reason of "noncompliance with DRS program.""

Kai started flipping through slides again. He began reading the names absently to himself. "Gilda Robinson... Trace Ruiz... Anthony Garrick..."

"I know that name," Hunter said.

"You worked with him, maybe?"

"No, no... it was the news..." Hunter pulled up his phone and did some frenzied tapping. "Here. Channel 5 News: 'Arlington Man Missing, Police Baffled.'"

"That other one you pulled up, Gilda Robinson..." Calhoun tapped on his computer keyboard. "Ward 6 in Boise forwarded us a BOLO from the local sheriff's department with that name."

"BOLO?" Hunter asked.

"Be on the Lookout," Kai explained.

"Here it is," Calhoun said, reading an email. "Gilda Louise Robinson, age 29. Missing, presumed endangered. May be in the Dallas-Fort Worth metro area."

"What's the DRS thing on her?" Hunter motioned for Kai to move the slide back.

"DRS status... engaged," Kai said. He moved the remote control back to Garrick. "Anthony's is marked 'engaged' too."

"Alright, so let's play 'What Do We Know," Calhoun said. "We know we have a list of 1,500 people who worked at InnerCore and who have since left the company."

"We know that a common thread among those that have left the company is that they accepted a vaccination as a condition of employment." Kai was making mental notes as he scanned the list of photos again.

"And we know that two of the people on this list have actually gone missing," Hunter said. "And their DRS status is 'Engaged,' whatever that means."

"And we know that there are three statuses," Calhoun said, reviewing his own notes. "Eligible, Ineligible, and Engaged.'"

"Four," corrected Kai with a lump in his throat.

"Four?" Calhoun and Hunter said in unison.

"Yeah, just found a fourth. 'Selected,'" Kai said.

"Who is marked as 'Selected?' asked Calhoun.

"Only two people, according to this list." Kai turned to them and clicked a button on the remote. Two employee ID's popped up, side-by-side.

"Alex Cavas... and Hunter Reeves."

6

PROBATIONARY STATUS

Averting his eyes, Hunter tried to avoid seeing the doctor approach with the needle that would enter his neck. "I thought vaccines were supposed to be given in the arm," he said as he winced in preparation for the shot.

"Normally, yes," said Dr. Kahn. "But we haven't been able to find a suitable vein in your arms, so we must try somewhere a bit more accessible."

"And this is supposed to protect me from what, again?"

"This is a special cocktail," Kahn explained, "of elements from the range of virulent samples we currently have at this facility. If any one or a combination of them were to be released, you should be protected if you came into contact with them."

The needle seared into his skin, just as he feared at would. Hunter sucked in his breath and pushed his neck further to the left as he waited for the pressure from the syringe being plunged in to subside.

"Sign this," said the doctor, thrusting a clipboard into Hunter's lap brusquely. "It's the completion form; give it to your direct supervisor to put in your file."

The clipboard also held a sterile bandage. Oh, Hunter reasoned, I suppose I have to put this on myself. He exited the doctor's office and tore the wrapper off the bandage, hastily pasting it to his neck.

A door opened and Dr. Kahn called after him. "Mr. Reeves! I forgot to advise you of possible side effects."

Hunter turned where he stood and looked at the doctor.

"Pain and redness at the injection site for up to ten days," said Kahn.

There was a pregnant pause.

"That's it?" Hunter prompted.

Dr. Kahn waited a moment more. "Yes."

He slammed the door shut.

Hunter woke from his dream, startled by the sound of a slam.

"Damn it!" He heard Kai shout from the kitchen area.

Rubbing his eyes, Hunter staggered from his bedroom and looked into the kitchen. Kai stood forlornly, holding a cookie tray holding six blackened, smoldering stones of what appeared to have once been biscuits. When he saw Hunter approach, he set the tray down sheepishly.

"I was gonna try to surprise you with breakfast in bed," he said sullenly.

"I see that," Hunter said, amused. He looked across the countertops to see opened packages of flour, a jug of milk, a carton of eggs, all de-shelled, and an empty pack of bacon. Following a hunch, he opened the garbage can to find puck after puck of blackened eggs and gray-and-black streaks of meat littering the can. "I appreciate the effort. Or the many efforts, in this case." He snickered.

"It's not funny!" Kai cried, wadding up the plastic that had held the raw bacon and tossing it in the opened bin.

"I think it is," Hunter said, still grinning.

Kai picked up a halved eggshell and lobbed it at Hunter. It bounced right off his forehead and split into more pieces as it hit the floor. "Okay, maybe it is," he said tauntingly.

"Brat," Hunter laughed, picking up the pieces and trashing them. Wiping his hands on his shirt he stepped close to Kai and tilted his head, planting a soft yet lingering kiss on his lips.

"So... last night wasn't weird? For you?" Kai asked nervously.

"I would have told you if it had been," Hunter offered. Kai nodded.

"A month and a half," Kai countered. "It wasn't rushing, but it wasn't an awful lot of time, either."

Hunter opened the fridge and passed Kai a bottle of blood, which he put in the microwave. Hunter saw Kai had bought him a few individual bottles of orange juice. He picked one up and opened it.

"It felt right," Hunter said. "Every moment of it. From the kiss to... everything else."

Kai nodded and waited for the microwave to finish before asking his next question. "Do you... would you want to move your things into my room... at this point?"

Hunter looked thoughtfully into his bottle before taking a swig. "What do I need to know? About how you sleep?"

"Well, you know by now I can do it at any point, day or night, as long as the room is light-tight." As he said this, Kai clicked a button on his smartphone app. The shutters to the living room began to open, displaying a dazzling view of the Dallas skyline. The sun had just set, leaving a breathtaking purple sky, with a few distant flashes of lightning from an approaching thunderstorm dotting through the clouds.

"I do prefer the room to be pretty cold when I rest," he continued. "Around 55 to 60 degrees."

Hunter whistled. "I can't begin to imagine your power bills in the summer," he said.

"Solar panels on the roof, m'dear," Kai grinned, pointing upward. "Usually in July and August I get refund checks from the power authority. *Anyway*," he said, alternating between sipping his bottle of blood and cleaning the counters, "I have plenty of blankets that you can use if you want. Other than that, sleeping with me will be fairly standard."

"What about the cat?"

"Annabelle?" Kai said, the name triggering the animal's senses. The calico trotted into the kitchen and nuzzled against Kai's right leg; in a figure-eight motion, she walked around his legs, then did the same to Hunter. "She's taken to you quite nicely. I don't think she'll mind you sharing her half of the bed.

"Her half. Sure." Hunter smirked.

Kai wiped the remaining flour from the countertop and tossed the rag in the sink. Hunter finished his bottle of juice, tossed it in the recycling bin next to the trash and embraced Kai. "Say it again," he whispered. "Just like you said it last night."

"Hunter," Kai said, nuzzling against his cheek. "I'm falling for you. I'm helpless to fight it. I well and truly believe I am in love with you."

"I love you too," Hunter replied.

Hunter waited to relay the details of his dream until they both went into the office that evening.

"Dr. Lawrence Kahn," Hunter said, having finally recalled the man's first name.

Kai typed the name into his computer. "There's no record of that name."

"I didn't just dream it up," Hunter said, "despite my remembering it through a dream."

"I don't doubt you, Hun," Kai replied. "I'm just saying, it isn't in any of the files we've recovered from Alex's computer and it's not in any of the publicly accessible files, either."

There was a knock at Kai's door. Agent Hayes, a tall and elegant looking woman of about 30 and flowing blond hair entered, carrying with her a load of magazines. "These are the medical journals we cross-referenced with mentions of InnerCore," she said, setting them on the coffee table in front of Hunter. "I warn you now - they're boring as all hell. Good luck!" She winked at them both before leaving.

Hunter took two magazines, put them in his lap, and turned the cover of both.

"You're not reading both at once, are you?" Kai peered over the edge of his desk.

"Not reading, exactly," Hunter said. "But I'm scanning the table of contents to see if I can find a direct mention or something InnerCore-related. If I can't, then I'll try actually reading these things." He tossed the first two aside and moved along to the next two.

"Meanwhile, there have been four more people to go missing off that list," Kai said. "Including a man who'd moved to Hawaii a week before he disappeared."

"Where's Alex?" Hunter replaced another pair of magazines.

"We've put him in a safe house," Kai said. "He think's we're CIA, and we're just going to let him think that."

"Has he said anything else that could be of use? Maybe I could talk to him or" –

Kai shook his head. "Between the paranoia he already had and the business that went down at the club, he was already on shaky ground."

Hunter looked confused. "He's not mentally stable right now, Hunter," said Kai. "If we're not careful, he could break completely."

"Oh."

There was an awkward silence that lasted several minutes, except for the occasional sound of Hunter discarding magazines and replacing them with others. Kai resumed work on his computer. After about ten minutes passed without the sound of papers changing positions from the sofa, Kai looked over at Hunter. He was staring at a single magazine.

"What is it?"

"It's this article about a technology being tested at InnerCore. Or it was. The FDA shut down this research project."

"Go on."

"'Indirect radiosynthesis,'" Hunter read, "was to be a radical form of cancer therapy by which, its researchers claimed, oncologists could inject into the body a barrage of laboratory-grown, healthy tissue cells programmed to instantly and rapidly replicate when introduced to a specific radio wavelength.

"The program's developers theorized they could essentially drive the healthy cells into the cancerous ones, destroying them, and replacing them with the self-replicating healthy tissue. The radio waves would then be shut off after a predetermined length of time, stopping the assisted growth of the healthy cells, and allowing them to grow at the body's normal rate."

"That sounds like a world-changing medical breakthrough," Kai said. "I hasten to ask, what caused the feds to cancel the project?"

Hunter shuddered. "According to this, in some tests on sample tumors, the radio waves had little control over the cells once they were turned on," he said. "In many cases they simply turned into tumors that grew ten times faster than the original cancer."

"Indirect radiosynthesis," Kai muttered. "What made it indirect?"

Hunter flipped a page. "Here's a diagram," he said, bringing the magazine over to Kai's desk. "It looks like a modified sonogram unit."

"Those things used to see the baby during pregnancy."

"Yeah. They hold the wand over the area of the body where the tumor is," Hunter indicated with his finger over the diagram. "And they use an ultrasonic wave to send the cells on their way to the tumor."

"So I guess my question is," Kai said, "if that was the *indirect* method… what would turn the process into a *direct* radiosynthesis… or a DRS?"

"That's gotta be what DRS stands for in that spreadsheet," Hunter concurred. "Well, if indirect meant holding the radio device over the body, I suppose the direct method would be having the radio… *in* the body." A chill ran down Hunter's spine. "Hun, am I able to access the medical records you all had me take when I joined up."

"Within reason - why?"

"I need to see my X-rays."

Moments later, Kai and Hunter were in the medical records office. Dr. Ife Mwodim slid her eyeglasses up her forehead as she leaned through the filing cabinet. Her English brogue was thick and charming. "You'd think only being here a short while, I could find your films quickly," she said. She looked up to smile gently at Hunter.

"Take your time," said Kai. He put a hand on Hunter's shoulder. "What are you thinking? What's that instinct telling you?"

"What if the research didn't stop at InnerCore?" Hunter posed. "What if it just continued, under the table? What if they moved on to another stage of the project?"

"Highly unethical, for starters," Kai said. "Plus, you're suggesting them putting an actual radio transmitter in the body. For the purposes you're suggesting it'd have to be microscopic. Molecular, even."

Dr. Ife made a noise - a cheer of success, then came up to the light box with a large manila folder. She tugged the X-ray films out of their sleeve. "Left side or right?"

Hunter recalled the moment in his dream again. "I was craning my neck to the left, so I guess the shot went into the right side of my neck."

The doctor slid the appropriate film under the clip of the light box and switched it on. All three of them strained to examine the bluish-white glow of bones on the film.

"I'm not seeing anything," Hunter said after a moment.

"Wait - I think I do," Kai said. "But... I don't know for sure. It could just be dust or a small nick in the X-ray plate."

"I have a digital copy on the mainframe," Dr. Ife suggested. "I'll pull it up on the monitor and zoom in."

"How powerful is the zoom feature?"

"Approximately 250 times," came the reply.

Hunter and Kai watched the large TV screen above Dr. Ife's desk as she called up the image and began the zoom.

"Shit," said Hunter.

"Oh, man," groaned Kai.

As the zoom reached its maximum setting, what Kai had hoped was a speck turned out to be exactly what they feared. There, embedded in Hunter's neck muscle, was a microscopic computer chip, complete with a transistor and at least three diodes, and a speaker the shape of an everyday shirt button.

"They put a friggin' radio in me," Hunter said.

"They put them in several hundred people," Kai said. "Including Alex."

Hunter gulped with dread. They had already learned those who were first reported missing had been 'engaged' in the DRS project.

And he and Alex had recently been 'selected' to join them.

7

VOLUNTEER OPPORTUNITIES

Dr. Ife put a comforting hand on Hunter's shoulder. He had been quivering and on the brink of tears since learning he had a microscopic radio transmitter lodged in his neck muscle for the better part of two years, and now he was being prepped in her office for its removal.

"Do you know what a biopsy is, dear?" Dr. Ife began to put on some surgical gloves.

"Y-yeah," said Hunter.

"Well, in some cases, the way it's done is the doctor will use a special punch-cutter, like this," and she held up a small, cylindrical steel device between her fingers, "to cut a small piece of skin from your body. We'll be doing much the same thing, but this one will be excising some of your muscle as well so we can retrieve the foreign body."

Hunter quaked. "Oh, ye gods," he shuddered.

"I understand," said Dr. Ife sympathetically. "It won't take very long though, and I'll be giving you a deep, local anesthetic. You shouldn't feel a thing."

Kai knocked on the office door and the doctor waved him in. He was holding a small vial with red liquid.

"A needle in my neck - again," bemoaned Hunter. "And a chunk of my body removed as well."

Kai brushed an errant lock of hair from Hunter's face as he smiled kindly at him. "Hey, it won't be that bad. You're not going to feel it. And it won't even leave a scar." He held up the vial so Hunter could see. "I haven't had a chance to tell you about this, but now seems a good a time as ever."

Hunter peered at it, rather than the instrument table Dr. Ife was setting up. "Looks like blood."

"It is - sort of," Kai said, grinning like a proud father. "This is probably the best thing our lab guys have ever developed. They call it 'Evermore.' It's a kind of synthetic vampire blood."

Dr. Ife tapped on her table with her folded eyeglasses. "Not that I'm after chasing accolades, but do let's remember who developed it before your 'lab guys' got to it, hm?"

Kai chuckled and winked at her. "Of course. I asked the good doctor here if she could create this masterpiece of biotechnology. See, Hun, vampire blood can do amazing things. It can help heal wounds incredibly fast - both ours and humans. In worst-case scenarios, we can even feed on it."

"Evermore is what I call a 'universal agent,'" the doctor added. "If needed, we can add vitamins, minerals, other medicines, to speed healing and recovery. Today, after I take the specimen from your neck, we will fill the wound with Evermore, and within five minutes, your neck will look like it does now."

Hunter looked genuinely impressed. "Wow," he said. Then he remembered he still had a date with a needle and a medical hole-puncher. "Well... let's just get this over with."

While Hunter sat on Kai's sofa in his office, looking over his completely-healed neck with a hand mirror, the doctor and Agent Myers, a red-headed lab technician with red-rimmed glasses, stood at Kai's desk going over the results of Hunter's procedure.

"It is indeed a radio transmitter," Myers said. "The good news is, it does not have any geo-positioning capabilities, so it isn't being used to track Hunter's location."

"That's a relief," Kai sighed. "That could have severely jeopardized us all."

"There was no sign of growing infection," Dr. Ife chimed in. "As far as I can tell, the device was created and kept in sterile conditions, then added into the solution they injected into Hunter. I have to assume it was the same for each patient.

"That's just it, though - they weren't patients. They were employees," Kai said. "They thought they were getting vaccinated - not becoming test cases."

The phone on Kai's desk began to ring. Myers and the doctor excused themselves. As they exited, Dr. Ife whispered to Hunter, "Hey there: You do him real wonders. He's not acted this lively in a long time. Keep it up!" She smiled and swept out of the office.

Hunter smiled to himself at her words. But the smile was short-lived.

"What?!" Kai yelled down the phone. "This is completely unacceptable! Where was the lookout?"

Hunter leapt to his feet and raced to Kai's side.

"Extend the perimeter and call in another crew to look with you all. I'm getting Calhoun." He slammed the receiver down and jumped from his chair. "Alex is gone."

"Gone!" Hunter followed behind Kai as he threw his office door open and marched toward Calhoun's office. "How could he be gone; I thought he was at a secured safe house!"

"Not secure enough, evidently," Kai growled. Hunter had not seen him this angry before. But as Kai spoke, Hunter could see a pair of fangs growing from two upper teeth.

"They think he escaped," Kai continued, "and if he has escaped in his mental state there's no telling what could happen."

After briefing Calhoun, the three of them piled into his car and drove out towards the safe house, just outside the city limits.

"Hunter, I want you to examine the house," Kai instructed. "You know the most about him; I want you to go over any of his possessions that might still be there. It could help us figure out where he went."

"Taylor, you and I are going to question the agents to see how this could have possibly happened," Calhoun said. His hands gripped the steering wheel. "This kind of laxity is incomprehensible."

They made their way to the safe house around 1 a.m. It was in a desolate area, about a mile from any neighboring structure. There was a wooded area to the left of the property, a small lake to the right. The three men popped out of the car and jogged to the home, where a milling throng of agents was gathered.

As instructed, Hunter made a beeline to the front door, opening it and striding inside. He took a long look at the open floorplan. Sofas in one corner, a bed in another, a kitchenette and a water closet-style bathroom and a privacy shower. Be it ever so humble, Hunter thought. He saw that the narrow window above the bed had been removed.

He walked to the kitchenette first, and opened the small fridge. There were several styrofoam takeout containers inside - the food within left untouched. There were empty containers of various beverages left on the counter. He was hydrating, at least, Hunter reckoned.

He walked slowly around the room, looking specifically for Alex's personal belongings. A few of his shirts were strewn about the floor, and a small suitcase lay on the bed, which had been haphazardly rifled through. Hunter stepped onto the mattress and leaned up to look out the window. He could see the pane of glass sitting neatly on the ground next to a patio chair.

Hunter sighed. Something wasn't right about that. He then gazed at the suitcase left on the bed. He sat down and started gingerly picking through some magazines and more clothing left inside.

He stopped when he saw the faintest glint of silver peeking over a pocket inside the suitcase.

Hunter exited the cabin and ran towards Calhoun and Kai, who were both questioning a female agent. She was standing at attention, hands clasped behind her back.

"Why wasn't the back porch being covered?" Calhoun asked.

"There had been a disturbance in the wooded area, sir," the agent said. Hunter tried to get a glimpse of her eyes, but between the darkness and the extended brim of her hat, he wasn't able to see. He did step closer, in part to watch her reactions, and part for the security of being close to Kai.

"What did you find when everyone got back to their stations?" Kai asked.

"We found the subject had vacated the premises," the agent replied. "I examined the back patio to find the window removed. I assume he used the disturbance as an opportunity for escape, sir."

"That's a load of crap," snapped Hunter. While Calhoun and Kai turned to look at him, the female agent remained at attention. Hunter unclenched one of his fists to reveal a silver chain with a rectangular locket attached to it. "This was Alex's mother's necklace," Hunter said. "It has the last photo they ever took together inside it. He always had it with him - even if he wasn't wearing it, he'd keep it in a pocket or somewhere near him. He'd never go anywhere without it."

He took a breath to keep his worry and anger in check. As he did, he saw some of the agent's fingers twitching. He also saw some light beginning to emanate in Kai's eyes. It was red. He was piecing something together, and it was making him angry.

"A-also," Hunter said, "the window. It's too far a drop for Alex to have removed it from the inside without dropping and breaking it. It's still in one piece next to a chair."

In a split second, a snarling Kai reached and grabbed the agent, yanking her by the lapels. Kai's eyes glowed ember red. "Agent, you had better start speaking, and truthfully. What happened to Alex?!"

Hunter watched the tension and rigidity melt away from the agent as Kai's influence took hold. His anger still clearly filled her with fear, as her response came out ragged and hesitant.

"He's right," she said. "I removed the window. I pulled him out during the diversion."

"Diversion," Calhoun grumbled. "Are you saying..."

"I was offered a great deal of money by a man in a van," the agent said, in a trance. "He gave me a pill to put in Alex's drink. Once he was asleep, he said he would cause a disturbance in the woods, to make the other agents investigate. Then I helped him take Alex out of the window. He said to make it look like he just... escaped."

Calhoun, infuriated, put a hand on his head in silence.

Kai, eyes still blazing, barked, "Where did you meet the man in the van? Where?!"

"In the woods, last night, during rounds," she said. As she continued to speak, Calhoun signaled to two other agents to put handcuffs on her. "But today I watched him carry Alex past the lake."

Hunter flinched. "He carried a fully-grown man on his own? How big of a man was *he?*"

"At least six-two," the agent said hazily. "Pretty bulky. Seemed to me he could easily break me in two if he wanted, that's why I felt obliged to take his offer."

"I'm done," Kai said. His eyes returned to their normal state and he let go of the agent's lapels. Her expression changed to one of confusion, then fear, then dismay as she discovered the handcuffs. She cried in protest as the other two agents led her away to a nearby vehicle.

Calhoun snapped his fingers, calling another pair of agents to him. "Check the area of the woods you all go through during rounds and look for any tire marks that would fit a large van," he said.

"Hunter and I will try and trace the man's path at the lake," Kai said. He took Hunter by the hand as they walked in that direction.

"Are-are you alright?" Hunter was unnerved by what had just transpired.

"I will be."

"What's going to happen... to her?"

Kai grumbled. "Best not to ask. You only get one chance with us. Betrayal is the one unforgivable sin."

Hunter let the words permeate the air as they continued in silence around the edge of the lake. Kai stopped when he noticed a footpath made through some tall grass. They began to follow the trail.

Hunter pulled out his phone and turned on the map application. "There's a road about a quarter-mile south from where we're at right now," he said.

"Look," Kai pointed. There was a pair of long curves dug through the grass before their feet. It had been freshly made. "Tire tracks. This was where the van peeled out."

"The guy had to be taking Alex back to InnerCore, right?" Hunter asked.

"It's our best guess for now unless we come up with new information," Kai admitted. "Let's go confer with Calhoun and get back to HQ."

In the car, Calhoun waited until he got the signal from Kai before rolling up the divider between the front and backseats.

"I need to make a confession," Kai said. His thumbs were twiddling.

"Oh?" A cold sensation ran down Hunter's back.

"Remember when I was talking to you about Evermore, and how we can mix it with just about any substance if it needs to get into the bloodstream?"

Hunter's eyes narrowed slightly, causing Kai a brief moment of panic. "Yes," Hunter said flatly.

"I, um, I added... a few drops... of my own blood to it."

Hunter seemed confused at the admission.

"Let me explain," Kai said quickly, defensively. "Since we're not kindred - uh, since I haven't made you a vampire... we don't have a bond. That is to say, I can't *track* you."

Hunter shook his head. "What? What are you trying to say?"

"A vampire and his progeny have a deep-seated bond between each other. One can know what the other is thinking, feeling, experiencing... they also know where the other is at all times. The only way a vampire and a mortal human can have that bond is if the human drinks some of the vampire's blood.

"I'm not about to ask you to do that," Kai continued. "But I need to have some way of knowing where you are. At least... temporarily. If we're ever separated during this investigation, knowing that you're wanted by InnerCore..."

"I get it," Hunter said. "If they take me, you'll know exactly where."

"Yes. I figured this would be the easiest way and least invasive way of doing that. Dr. Ife told me the effect would only last a few weeks, a month at most. I-I'm sorry," Kai said. "I know I should have told you beforehand."

Hunter nodded. "Yes, you should have." He took a deep breath and took both of Kai's hands. "You can't do that to me again," he said, sternly. "Not if we're going to be partners in this. Not if we're going to be lovers. Alex withheld so much from me in the past, and it looks like it's starting to come back on me. No matter if you think it's for my benefit or my safety, or what--do *not* hold back from me ever again. Am I clear on that?"

Kai bit his lower lip and nodded.

"Besides, if this is truly going to help you keep tabs on me, it makes this even easier to suggest," Hunter said. "If the key to this, if the most important thing now is figuring out where all these missing people are, I figure the easiest way to do that is... to go missing myself."

Kai opened his mouth but couldn't find the words. "What?"

"I realized at the cabin. The windows," Hunter said with a sad smile. "That window had already been unbolted and ready to take down. Both there... and at the club. Whether it was Alex or me or maybe even both of us..."

"Someone had known one or both of you would be in or near the club that night," Kai finished.

"Any number of our coworkers knew we went there all the time," Hunter said. "It would have been easy for whoever's behind this to just set a trap if they knew we'd be there."

"They just hadn't counted on The Order running an operation the same night," Kai added. "Tell me," he said. "Do the initials D.K. mean anything to you?"

"D. K.," Hunter repeated. "Not off the top of my head, no."

"When Messinger, that guy we were targeting at the club, was being interrogated, he told Mugan he was 'acting under orders from D.K.,' but we never got further than that. Messinger didn't seem to know who D.K. worked for. We still don't know why Alex was trying to sell Messinger the InnerCore DRS list."

Hunter thought for awhile. "Doctor Kahn... Could 'D.K.' be Doctor Kahn?"

"The guy that gave you the injection? It's possible," Kai said. "But why, then, would Messinger be buying an InnerCore list for the doctor who works at InnerCore?"

There was a pause. "Maybe Alex had been doing his own detective work," Hunter suggested. "If he'd hacked into InnerCore and taken that one document, there had to have been more. Perhaps he was trying to stop Inner-Core from doing this once he learned people were going missing."

"It's a good theory, but we're going to need solid proof. There wasn't much on Alex's computer to connect those dots," Kai said.

"That's why I need to go back," Hunter said. "That's why I've got to get back into InnerCore."

8

CROSS-TRAINING

Hunter hadn't been able to sleep since volunteering to go back to his former workplace, where the investigation had led them to believe some sort of illegal testing on humans was happening. Kai and Calhoun were still planning a course of action for the operation, but the thought was still keeping Hunter up. Since moving in with Kai, he had been able to sleep at the same hours the vampire took - dawn to dusk. But it was midday and he was wide awake. He turned the bedroom lights on to get dressed. Kai had moved some clothes out of his sleek onyx chest of drawers for Hunter. Half of everything, in fact - the dresser, the closets. All of Kai's space had been split in half for their shared quarters.

Hunter put on another T-shirt depicting one of his favorite bands, a Finnish group called Poets of the Fall. Their symbol, a giant moth, a pin stuck through its body, wrapped from the middle of the shirt's front to the center of the back. It was meant to encourage people to "seize the day," since you never know when that life may change or end.

He glanced over at the bed, where Kai lay in deep sleep. Hunter crept closer and examined his lover's body. In daylight, with Kai literally dead to the world, his skin looked pale and ashen. The skin around his cheekbones and eyes had sunken down slightly. Hunter could see purple shadows of veins streaking down Kai's arms and face, spread out like tree limbs. It wasn't necessarily a pleasant look compared to the lively, spry, slightly tanned look Kai sported when he was active.

For one terrible moment, Hunter felt a twinge of disgust, followed instantly by regret. This isn't *him*, he reminded himself. It's just his body, recharging. One in a series of adjustments Hunter was having to learn to understand.

One day, he reasoned, he may decide he would want to spend eternity by Kai's side. He wouldn't see this side of him - the daylight version - again if that were the case. He'd also never see sunlight again, he thought. Or see animals who thrived in daylight.

Maybe today would be a good day to take those sights in again, and to cherish them. To seize the day.

He wondered if it would be possible to wake Kai up to see if he could walk around his property. He knelt by the bedside and gently nudged Kai's arm.

It felt leathery and wrinkled. It jarred Hunter. He moved his hand to push at Kai's shoulder, which was covered by a T-shirt.

"Kai," Hunter whispered. "Kai. Wake up for a moment."

Kai stirred. He groaned, an almost pained creaking noise. "Hunter? Isssssomething wr-r-rong?"

"No. I just wanted to know if it's okay for me to take a walk outside for a bit?"

"Uhhhh, ssssure," Kai said, his eyes so heavy he couldn't lift them. "Just enter-r-r-r the code when you go in and out. And stayyyy on the property. Th....the guards won't... bother you..." And he fell back into a dead sleep.

Hunter reached for his travel bag that still had odds and ends. He found a small tube of sunscreen still there. He slathered some on his arms, face, and neck. With it nearing the height of summer in Texas, the sun was notoriously brutal. If there was a plus side to never seeing the sun again, it would be the risk of sunburn and heatstroke.

He entered the security code on the panel by the front door and stepped outside and looked out onto the property.

The home, while modern and technologically advanced in every way inside, looked like an old-style Texas ranch house on the outside. Limestone columns, a poured concrete porch, and treated wood features enveloped the outer walls. The steps opened to a beige gravel path that led the quarter-mile or so to the gate, where Hunter could see two guards wearing white cowboy hats, lightweight shirts and blue denim jeans stationed. To the few who might pass by the otherwise secluded road, it would seem this was an everyday farm.

There was a large cane leaning by the front door. He figured he could use it as he strolled, passing it in front of him in case there were any snakes in the grass he couldn't see. Hunter walked a few paces down the gravel road. To his left, he admired a large oak tree, its large, heavy branches arching over a small duck pond. He took the cane and passed it in front of him, left and right, as he neared the pond.

Grasshoppers leapt as the cane struck the ground, and Hunter had to recoil and swat a few out of his face. Normally he would have fled back into the house rather than face any insect, but this time he just waved them by.

He took a seat against the trunk of the giant tree. He examined the lush green grass leading up to the bank of the pond, and saw where it gradually turned yellow and brown in the open sun.

It was the sun baking the ground that Hunter noticed he could smell. He took several deep breaths. It was a mixture of the fresh grass and the crisped, parched earth just a few paces beyond, swirling together into this extraordinary scent.

Grasshoppers again - the sound! Thousands of them, across the property's many acres, sounding off, rattling, chirping as they moved about. He'd never truly appreciated their symphony.

Hunter took out his phone and pulled up the camera app. He turned the phone on its side and pointed it towards the house. He let it record video, so it would pick up the sounds of this moment, and the sights of the sun bathing everything in this warm glow, sparkling off the water of the pond, and being absorbed by the solar panels checkerboarded across the roof of Kai's house.

Their house.

The more Hunter thought of the house as theirs, his life as theirs, the more he realized that sacrificing daylight would be a small price to trade for his companion, his partner, and his true love.

An hour later, he was able to walk back into the house, have a quick shower, and crawl back into bed, falling fast asleep with his arm around Kai's waist.

They met in Calhoun's office that night to discuss the final plan for infiltrating InnerCore.

"We figure the easiest course of action would be for you to reapply for work," Calhoun said.

"Makes sense," Hunter agreed. "I left on good terms; I just said that my financial situation had changed and I didn't need the work. I lied, but it left me with a way back in if I needed it."

"Good," said Calhoun.

"We're going to list your address as Alex's apartment," Kai said cautiously. "Are you going to be alright staying there, if necessary? We figure that's going to ring some alarm bells with Kahn."

Hunter nodded. "I guess. We've decided Kahn is running the show then?"

"InnerCore essentially went out of business when the FDA nixed the radiosynthesis plan," Calhoun said, looking through a dossier filled with documents. "They sold the name and the deed to the property to Kahn for pennies on the dollar."

"Wait," Hunter interrupted. "If they're not really operating anymore, why am I going in as a job applicant?"

Calhoun cleared his throat in slight annoyance at being interrupted. "As I was going to say, we figure that with you essentially offering yourself up to him, he would 'make' a position open and bring you inside immediately." Hunter bit his lower lip and nodded, very aware of his superior's irritation.

"Messinger was his number two," Calhoun continued. "We finally pieced together that he was orchestrating the abductions of those selected to continue with the DRS program. We now know that the offer to buy the document from Alex was just a ruse and Alex was indeed going to be abducted that night in the alley. "

"Now Kahn has to shoulder the load himself, and we assume he'll want you to be his 'medical assistant,' so to speak... until he needs you for his own purposes later," Kai said, taking a printout from Calhoun and handing it to Hunter to see.

It was a grainy security photo of Kahn. Hunter recognized the face. What looked different from the Kahn of his recollection was how much bigger he seemed. He looked like a bodybuilder. He was at least four inches taller than Hunter remembered. Intimidating, if Hunter were to summarize it in one word.

"We need to assume you're going to come into contact with him right away," Calhoun said. "And at that point, you're likely to be brought to wherever the others are being held. It's important that you do *not* fight it. Be agreeable, but don't be a pushover either."

"Maybe... hesitate a bit, ask 'why' a few times, then go where I'm told, do what I'm told," Hunter said.

"Exactly. I don't think he'll ask you to harm anyone yourself. Our profilers are quite certain Kahn is savoring all the grotesque pleasure he gets in doing... whatever he's doing... for himself. Now, this is where things get a bit hairy," Kai said. "Kahn might let you go that first day.

But expect that he will make it clear you're not leaving the building at some point. As long as you're agreeable and not combative, he may let his guard down and you must use any opportunity to get evidence. SD cards, USB's, paper, anything."

"What do I do with it when I find it?"

"Stash it," Calhoun replied. "Anywhere you'll be able to find it later. If it's in your sock or clothes, great - but be prepared to hide it somewhere else in the facility. If you can't get to it again, we might be able to find it later."

"'We?' 'Later?'"

Kai took a labored look at Hunter. "While you're gone, I'm going to work with my team to figure out a way to infiltrate. Hopefully by the first day; no later by the second. They would give you a signal, some sign that we're there. And you could potentially hand off evidence to them. But we also need to discuss 'Plan X.'

"Which already sounds nice and cheery..."

"A worst-case scenario," said Calhoun. He produced a thin tube of paper, bound in red ribbon. "The Order protocol dictates that you read this document in full and sign your name to it, right now, before you start this mission."

A twinge of despair coursed through Hunter's body. He looked at Kai, who nodded back, solemn faced. Hunter took the paper from Calhoun, untied the ribbon, and uncurled the document.

The paper was brown, almost like aged parchment. In heavy, blue calligraphy, was a block of text, which Hunter read aloud:

"The following, by special decree of The Order, is a conditional authorization for Agent Hunter Reeves to locate, gather evidence against, question, and, if necessary... terminate... one Dr. Lawrence Kahn, aged 48.

"Objective - admission of guilt for crimes against humanity including false imprisonment, medical testing without express consent, and egregious bodily harm. Conditions in which termination will be authorized include, and are solely limited to, imminent danger or threat of death against said Agent... Or imminent danger or threat of death against any informant or subject confiding critical information to Agent in the course of his investigation."

Hunter held the scroll to his side and looked at Kai and Calhoun. "So what does this mean, exactly?"

"It means, for starters, that you need to try and speak with any of the other test subjects and get them to talk about what they're experiencing. The language of the scroll is written loosely enough that if you can get any first-hand account, it will count as evidence."

"It also means that you can't just go in and kill him," Kai explained. "And there will be a certain .. threshold .. that he must cross before you even think about trying to."

"Such as?"

Calhoun set the dossier down and walked behind his desk. "You may have to let him inject you again."

Hunter bristled.

"We have to assume it to be an eventuality," Kai explained. "He's not got you marked for some test to not inject you with something.'

As Hunter tensed further, Kai rushed to his side, holding him gently by one arm. "Think of it this way," Kai said. "I know the stress the thought of injections gives you. That should be enough for me to pinpoint exactly where you are, and I can come and get you, and end him, so you don't have to."

"But he has to clearly, verbally indicate he intends to harm you," Calhoun advised, "or any of his other subjects, before you even think of eliminating him."

"I don't *want* to think about eliminating him!" Hunter shouted. "How can I? Look at him - he's a Hulk! I'd never be able to pull it off!"

"Then think about how to fend him off," Kai said. "Go on the defensive. Run. Throw things, pull things down to create obstacles to block him. Then hide."

"We're not saying these things are *going* to happen," Calhoun added. "But we have to prepare you for any circumstance. The conditional authorization to kill is a last resort. In case Kai can't get to him first."

"That's right, Hun," Kai said. "If all goes right, that'll be my responsibility. You'll have gathered all the proof, and that's all I need to do my job." He held up his own scroll, tied with red ribbon, just like Hunter's had been.

"I guess this is what I signed up for," Hunter said. There was a pit in the depths of his gut as he held out his right hand. "Somebody give me a pen."

The rest of that evening's shift was spent with the three men going over every possible scenario they could come up with, followed by a possible response Hunter might be able to perform.

With a half an hour to go before sunrise, Hunter and Kai returned home. Hunter was visibly, understandably nervous. Even Annabelle was aware of it. As the two men sat at the foot of their bed, the cat leapt up and rested her head gingerly on Hunter's thigh, purring heavily. He absently stroked her head.

"I know how anxious you have to be feeling," Kai said. "But I believe in you. You've got this."

"We have absolutely no idea what kind of 'this' I'll be walking into," Hunter countered. "All the planning and 'what if' scenarios we came up with could be worthless once I get inside."

"True, but," Kai said, tenderly taking one of Hunter's hands and clasping it tightly in his, "I've watched how you work these past months. Even when it's combing through paperwork or walking through an apartment, you have a knack for picking up details. You think logically, but you allow for the unorthodox. And that's what you're going into - a strange, unorthodox situation. As long as you keep that situational awareness about you... I think you'll do fine."

Hunter saw the slightest of twitches in Kai's eyes as he spoke. "And you're not worried about what will happen."

"I'm petrified," Kai said with a small, sad smile. "But there's precious little I can do about it until night falls again. Which reminds me, do you have the anklet the lab made?"

"Yeah." Hunter lifted his right leg. An anklet that appeared to be made of braided brown leather strips hung gently at the ankle.

"Good. Remember, it's an impact-sensitive beacon. Inside one of the braids is a gyroscope that measures your pace. If you happen to get into a scrape of some sort - fall down, hit something - it'll go off and transmit a silent panic signal to HQ. They'll mobilize the team getting set up near the InnerCore building."

"Right," Hunter said. "Love... you'll be going to sleep here in a few and I'll be heading off to InnerCore. Could we just spend it... quietly?"

Kai nodded. His features were already going dull and the shadow of his veins began to appear. He shifted up in the bed and got under the covers. Hunter got up to set the thermostat to Kai's preferred sleep temperature... 58 degrees. He then rounded the bed and climbed onto his side, wrapping an arm around Kai. They laid there, embracing in silence until Kai had succumbed to his death-sleep. Hunter gently climbed out of bed again. He looked at his phone. 8 a.m.

He crossed to the bedroom door, turning out the lights as he opened the door. He took a final look at his partner, resting peacefully in bed.

"I hope I see you again, love," he whispered, more to himself than to Kai. "Sooner, rather than later."

9

EMPLOYEE OF THE MONTH

Hunter arrived at the golden-veneered InnerCore building at 9 a.m. sharp. All markings of the company's logo had been removed, and as he pulled the handle to the entrance door, he found it locked. But as he peered inside, he could see there was someone at the reception desk. Seeing a buzzer with an intercom by the handle, he pressed it.

"Yes?" The voice of the woman at the desk crackled in a way that instantly offended the ear.

"Uh, yes. Um, I've come to see about applying for a job?"

"Sorry, we're not hiring," the voice wasn't unfriendly, just crisp.

"Does Dr. Kahn still work there, by any chance?"

There was a brief pause. "He does," the woman replied. "But he's quite busy."

"I'm sure he'd want to see me," Hunter said. "Would you page him, please? Tell him Hunter Reeves would like to see him."

Another pause. "Hold, please."

Hunter waited patiently at the door, checking his reflection in the mirrored glass of the entrance. For a moment he felt as if he were really a job applicant. He jumped slightly when the door opened and the receptionist motioned for him to come inside.

The foyer looked just like Hunter remembered it; green marble over every square inch, but all evidence of an operating business had been removed, save for the receptionist's desk. No waiting room furniture, no TVs playing the local cable news channel softly in the background. Again, the brass logo announcing to the world this was "InnerCore Industries… Progress Brings Us Together," had been pried from the walls, leaving the faintest of scars on the marble.

"Dr. Kahn will be with you shortly," the receptionist said. She tousled her curly, black hair and straightened the hem on her blouse as she walked back behind her desk. "My apologies for the wait, as I said, we weren't actually expecting anyone today. May I get you some water?"

"Oh, uh, yes, please," Hunter stammered. Anything to keep himself calm, he figured.

The receptionist filled a mug with water from a desktop dispenser and offered it to Hunter, who took it and began drinking immediately. He set the mug on the desk just as a large set of double-doors behind the desk opened. They hissed as their air-lock disengaged, almost heralding the person behind them to step forward.

"Mr. Reeves, what a surprise," said a deep, disaffected voice. Dr. Kahn breezed past the doors. He was just as imposing as Hunter had seen in the dossier, yet nowhere near how he remembered. Kahn's hair had been buzzed short, and he was indeed much more muscular and taller than when Hunter had first been hired.

"Dr. Kahn," was all Hunter could think to say.

"What brings you here," Kahn asked, breaking the silence.

"I had, uh, come here asking about possibly returning to the data entry department," Hunter said. He tried to remain calm, as instructed. "I had no idea InnerCore had closed down."

"Not closed," Kahn said, removing his glasses, taking a small cloth from his lab coat pocket and cleaning the lenses. "We have changed our focus recently, and as such we decided it was best to trim our personnel down to the... barest of essentials."

"Oh. I see," Hunter pretended to be disappointed. "I'm terribly sorry to have wasted your time."

"Well, you might not have," Kahn said, replacing his spectacles. "As it happens, I am in need of a lab assistant. If you are interested, of course. There's no prior experience needed. Just grunt work, mostly, though there is a chance you could help me with some procedures down the line. Would you be interested?

Hunter forced a grateful smile. "Yes! Certainly."

Kahn pursed his lips in what Hunter assumed was his display of a smile. "Splendid," he said, spinning on his heels. "Right this way. Nancy? The door."

The receptionist pressed a button at her desk, causing the doors to hiss and unlock, opening to their fullest extent. Hunter followed Dr. Kahn down the hallway.

Here we go, he thought, another point of no return.

"You've never seen this wing of the building," Kahn said, hands behind his back, strolling slowly past a bright white corridor. "Allow me to give you a quick tour."

As he stayed two paces behind Kahn, Hunter made note of hallmarks of each passageway. Each office, each door they passed looked identical. There was no sign or nameplate attached. He also noticed a security camera here and there... but the indicator light on each camera was dark, meaning they likely weren't recording.

Kahn stopped at another set of double doors. "So let me explain what we're doing," he said. We have a small number of patients with us for an extended period. They each have some form of cancer, you see, and we're testing an advanced form of therapy on them. One of your chief duties will be to check on them every two hours and prepare, serve, and clean up after their meals."

"Cancer," Hunter echoed. "How horrible."

"Yes. A terrible malady," Kahn said, without a hint of compassion in his voice. He opened the door and held it for Hunter to pass through first.

As his eyes adjusted from the bright lights of the hallway to the dim, nearly useless light in this new room, Hunter could see this large room was filled with 16 hospital beds. Nine of them were empty, the others had their curtains wrapped around, indicating someone was in them.

There was carpet on the floor, Hunter noticed. That seemed odd. Any hospital ward he'd ever been to had tile. This is makeshift, Hunter realized. More cameras in each corner of the room, he saw - and each powered off.

"We have someone on staff who helps them get up and out of bed for their ablutions," Kahn continued, whispering quietly and continuing on a beeline across the room to the next set of doors. "I perform their treatments. And you will, as I said, prepare their food. For privacy's sake, I ask that you do not open the curtains. Just lay the trays out on the tables next to their beds and carry on to the next."

"Noted," Hunter said.

"The kitchen is right through here," Kahn said, pushing past the next set of doors. Hunter followed dutifully behind.

While there was a refrigerator and microwave, like he expected for a kitchen, they were normally-sized. Instead of a stove or an oven, there was a single hot plate on a counter. This was a break room, Hunter thought, not something meant to prepare food for hospital patients.

"Everything you need for a meal is in the cabinets and the fridge," Kahn said. "One item per meal per person, please. And that includes you," he added, with another tight-lipped smile.

"Me?" Hunter panicked but tried not to let it show.

"Yes. Your meals will be on us, free of charge to you. Consider it a perk of the job."

"Oh! Uh, sure," Hunter said, nodding.

"Any questions thus far?" Kahn asked.

"How much?"

The question caught the doctor off guard. "Pardon?"

"Um, how much... per hour?" Hunter put his hands in his pockets. "I kinda hit a rough patch, I just need to make sure what I'm making is worth it, you know?"

Kahn nodded. "I understand. How much did you make when you were with us before?"

"Fourteen an hour," Hunter replied.

"Let's add a dollar to that," Kahn said. "Will that suffice?"

Hunter could tell Kahn was bullshitting. Money was not going to factor into this, as far as the doctor was concerned. This was just to appease Hunter and keep him from leaving. He smiled in false gratitude. "That would be great - when can I start?"

"Would you have any qualms about starting immediately?"

"Not at all!"

"Right," Kahn said crisply. "Follow me, we shall get you a lab coat."

"I'll be done at five, is that right?" Hunter asked a few minutes later, decked out in a starched, bleached, sanitized lab coat.

"Actually," Kahn said as he reclined in his office chair, "and I apologize for already asking favors of the new employee, but would you be amenable to staying overnight?"

"Overnight?" Hunter furrowed his brow.

"Yes. You see, there is a lot of disused furniture that needs to be put upstairs in storage, and it must be done by morning for the liquidators to take stock of. I simply have too much to do," Kahn said, patting a large stack of papers in folders on his desk. "You'll get overtime, of course."

"Oh, uh, that's not a problem," Hunter began, "um, but would there be some time for me to perhaps get a nap in?"

"Certainly," Kahn said, feigning a kind smile. You'll be moving plenty of chairs. And, of course, there's the sofa here in my office. I assure you I won't mind if you need to lay your head there for an hour or two. So long as the task at hand gets done."

Hunter spent the next three hours hauling rolling chairs out of the empty offices, scuttling them into the service elevator and into the room above. The room was expansive, but apart from a large bank of unwieldy and heavy boxes placed in one corner of the room, it was empty and waited to be filled with more junk.

His muscles were aching and burning; it was the most physical activity he had undertaken in quite some time. After exiting the elevator to the ground floor for what seemed like the fiftieth time, Hunter crossed the hallway to the break room-cum-kitchen. He slid into the lone leather reading chair stashed there, folded his arms on the small fast food restaurant-style table, and rested his head.

"I gotta get outta here!" The pleading shout of a voice coming from the makeshift hospital ward beyond the doors made Hunter snap to attention. He recognized the voice immediately. It was Alex.

"Alex?" He rose from the chair and started for the door leading to the hospital beds.

As soon as he placed his hands on the door to push it forward, the one leading to the kitchen swung open. "What're you doing?" Dr. Kahn's voice grated like razor wire.

Hunter spun to face him. No need to lie at this point, he reckoned. "I was resting and heard a voice," he said.

Kahn stepped to Hunter and put a hand on his shoulder. It was a tight grip, unnecessary for the situation, Hunter thought. "No need to concern yourself," Kahn said. "It's the sedation wearing off. That patient's condition is... quite advanced. But that's my cross to bear," he said. He felt around in his pocket until he found and produced a pre-filled syringe.

Uncapping it and heading for the hospital door, Kahn gave Hunter an unsettling look. "Please. Tend to your duties, and await my further instructions."

"Yes, sir."

"By the way," Kahn said, using his posterior to push the door open slightly. "Did you ever experience any undue side effects from the vaccination we gave you the last time you were with us?"

Hunter shook his head with a nervous grin. "Uh, no," he said. "Never felt a thing after that first day or so. Just like you said."

Kahn nodded, then fully entered the hospital ward, letting the door close behind him.

Hunter hurriedly left the kitchen and ran into the hallway. He rested his head against the wall, breathing heavily. Alex was in there, for sure. He had to see what condition he and the others were in, but he'd have to wait until Kahn gave him permission to be in the ward. Probably mealtime.

It pained him to not be able to act immediately. But he had to obey not only Kahn, but the mission agenda, which meant doing as instructed for now. That meant trying to locate evidence.

He crossed the hall to Kahn's office. He had enough time to at least do a visual scope. Maybe look at the first two or three documents on the stack on the doctor's desk.

Hunter cautiously opened and closed the door to prevent any noise, then crept over to the desk. He opened the flap of the folder on top of the stack and scanned for any important-looking words.

"Good God," he muttered to himself. "This is what he's trying to do? He's insane..."

The clacking of the doctor's shoes coming from the hallway alerted him to move. He closed the folder, dashed to the side door by the doctor's sofa, and entered the adjoining room, closing the door just before the main office door swung open.

"Hunter?" Kahn barked.

"In here!" Hunter called cheerfully from the next room. Spotting two rolling chairs tucked inside a desk, he swiftly grabbed them both by the headrest, then opened the front door to the spare office.

"These are the last from this hall," Hunter said, pushing the chairs to a stop inches from Kahn's legs. "I'm just about to store 'em upstairs with the rest.

Kahn eyed Hunter up and down with a wary eye. "I see," he said defeatedly. "Well. Very good. You've worked very hard so far."

"Thanks," Hunter said. Sweating, he wiped his brow. "It's very hot work, too!"

"Here," Kahn said. He pulled a handkerchief from his pants pocket and handed it absently to Hunter. He accepted it and wiped his forehead. A strong odor wafted from the cloth, causing Hunter to take it away from his face immediately, reflexively putting it in his pocket.

"I need to leave the building for an hour or two," Kahn said. "With our delivery contracts ended, I must go pick up my own orders of medical supplies. Since you've wrapped up with the chairs, I'd like for you to move on to packing up any leftover decorations or items left in the desks. They can be placed in the incinerator on the third floor."

"Very good, sir."

"Remember, mealtime is at 2 p.m.," Kahn added as he grabbed a set of keys from the same pants pocket. "Remember our rules about serving the patients. I shall be back by 3."

Hunter nodded dutifully and allowed Kahn to pass by him and the chairs on his way out through the reception area. He pushed the chairs quickly to the elevators and pushed the call button. Chewing on his thumbnail, he plotted his course of action for the next two hours.

When the elevator doors opened to the storage floor, Hunter rolled the chairs with a firm push, letting them stop haphazardly to the clean end of the room. Hunter trotted to the window overlooking the city street and peeked through one of the closed Venetian blinds. He watched as a large white van passed underneath, turning the corner leading to the freeway.

Hunter glanced over at the far end of the storage room, where the wall of boxes stood. To the right, where the boxes ended, he could see a large surge protector strip plugged into the wall. Curious, he crossed to the bank of heavy boxes and started to wiggle a column apart from the others so he could see past them.

It was a control deck, he could see: an elongated corner desk with four... five.. *six* small, old-style television screens. This room must have been the security department, Hunter reckoned. Encouraged, Hunter wrestled with a few more stacks of boxes until he could forge a path towards the desk. Hoping for the best, he flipped one of the televisions on.

It took a moment for the machine to warm up, but eventually a picture of static came into view. Hunter quickly flipped all the TVs on and let them get to the point of displaying static. Next step, Hunter thought... figure out how to get the security cameras on. He let his hand snake around the first television set he could reach, into the recessed cabinetry, until it hit upon a series of dials. He turned it one click to the right. The TV picture changed immediately to an image of the hallway adjoining Kahn's office.

Yes! Hunter immediately began pushing the other columns of boxes aside to give him more room to maneuver. In doing so, the top box from one stack toppled over, and a bunch of smaller black boxes crashed to the floor.

Ignoring them for the moment, Hunter was able to reach to the control dial for each television, turning them until he was able to select a range of cameras - two from the hospital ward, one from the hallway Kahn had used to lead Hunter to the hospital ward, and another from the reception area looking toward the front entrance. He looked at his options for the final camera. Dr.

Kahn's office came up first. A good idea, Hunter reasoned, but I'd better look further. Clicking the dial a few more times, an area Hunter had not yet seen came into view: another carpeted area, obviously intended for some other purpose, but this one filled with a doctor's exam table. He recognized it as the one he'd sat on getting his so-called "vaccination."

But this room was laid out differently. There were several minifridges against one wall. There was a table laid out with instruments and devices he couldn't recognize. Hunter figured this one would be more important that Kahn's office.

He knelt to the floor to examine the desk area. There were two areas for chairs to be kept, which were occupied by boxes. Next to each, a locked cabinet door. He put his ear to one door and could hear a very faint hum. More equipment, but what?

Jumping to his feet, he scanned the walls of the empty security office. On the wall next to the elevator door was a bulletin board with a cup. He ran up to the bulletin board and examined the cup. Inside was a bevy of push-pins and paper clips.

He checked the flip-clock mounted above the bulletin board. It flipped from 12:59 PM to 1:00 PM.

He took a few paper clips and rushed back to the equipment console. Unbending the wire clips, he started working to jimmy the cabinet door open. It took a few minutes, but he was able to get the lock disengaged. He flew the door open. Inside, he found three videotape recorders, marked 4-6.

Tapes. He scrambled on the floor towards the black boxes he'd knocked over. Opening one, he saw a large videotape cassette. He peered through the plastic window of the cassette, and saw the tape had never been used. He grabbed two more of the cassette cases and hurriedly set each one into a machine, jabbing the 'Record' button once the tape loaded. A red light illuminated on the recorder and began blinking, indicating recording had started.

He picked up the paper clips and began working on opening the second cabinet.

A chime sounded, startling Hunter, who looked towards the source - the clock. It was 1:30 already. In order to get the patients' food set up by 2, he'd have to get back downstairs now. Maybe he could get back to the other machines later. He switched each TV monitor off and closed the cabinet doors to muffle the recorders' noise. He did his best to get the boxes set back up the way they were, then rushed downstairs.

Hunter had his cart loaded with six trays, each containing a single-serve container of cereal, an apple, and a heated container of instant macaroni and cheese. Taking a deep breath, he backed into the door leading to the hospital ward.

Beginning at the far end of the room, Hunter crept next to each bed and gingerly placed a tray of food on the serving table. At first, he did as instructed and avoided opening the curtains. Then, as he approached the third occupied bed, he looked up and realized the camera pointing at the bed had its indicator light blinking. It was recording!

Being as quiet as possible, Hunter slowly drew the curtain back. Laying in this bed was a woman, likely in her forties, sleeping deeply. They were likely all drugged to stay asleep during Kahn's absence. Hunter slowly picked up her right arm to examine it. Instead of skin pigmented like the rest of her body, this arm was as green as grass, and textured like alligator scales. The discoloration and started at her bicep and got stronger as it moved down her arm, where at about the crook, the scales began. Her hand was forest green, with skin exactly like a gator... and claws where the fingernails should have been.

Hunter shuddered. This was exactly what the file he examined in Kahn's office described.

Alex. He had to see if Alex's file was as accurate as Mrs. Robinson's.

Remembering the time limit he faced, he quickly set Gilda Robinson's arm back to her side and pulled the curtain back. He hoped that camera had picked up enough detail of her mutated arm.

He made his way to the last bed, dutifully placing food trays along the way. Rather than open the curtain, he decided to just peek his head behind it.

Alex lay there, also heavily sedated. His olive-skinned chest was clearly visible... as was the purple, baseball-sized growth over his right pectoral muscle. It throbbed violently, veins protruding and inflamed.

Hunter had to suppress the urge to retch. He looked directly at the camera facing Alex's bed. While the camera's light was on, it was not blinking. It would not be recording.

As he heard the air lock of the doors down the hallway activating, he knew Dr. Kahn had returned. He hurriedly gathered his serving cart and bustled it back into the kitchen area.

Walking back towards the office corridor, Hunter went over the things he had just done. The security tapes will be great evidence, he knew. The tapes had been marked for 12 hours of recording time. And if nothing else, he had Mrs. Robinson's arm on tape to satisfy the proof requirement of the scroll.

He needed to get some for Alex, though. If he couldn't get the camera pointed at his bed to record, he'd need a backup idea.

Hunter needed to find Alex's old desk.

10

DEADLINES

With there being little hope of getting to question Alex and the other captives - between being sedated and Dr. Kahn always ready to give them more injections when they began to cry out - Hunter was going to have to rely on the tape recordings and any other evidence he might be able to procure.

He had a hunch that Alex might have done what he'd done at his apartment, tape something under his desktop at work... but Hunter had to locate it.

After taking two boxfuls of odds and ends from the offices to the incinerator, Hunter came back to the ground floor and went to the last office nearest the reception desk. Flipping on the light switch, he gazed over the dozen or so desks crammed to one side of the room. One desk immediately stuck out - laminated to its top was a yearly calendar with a sports emblem, a thick green circle with the letter A on it. The Oakland A's was Alex's favorite baseball team.

Hunter saw he could go underneath the first row of desks and be able to see under the second row perfectly easily. He did so, then strained to reach for Alex's desk, which was against the wall.

He saw two USB sticks clearly underneath a hastily-torn piece of cellophane tape. It took a few more reaches, but Hunter was able to grasp the tape and yank it free. Holding the tape under the light, he could see there were labels on each thumb drive. One was marked 'My PC.' The other was labeled 'CANDCEXE."

Without time to figure out what that might mean, Hunter put the tape with the drives still attached and stuck it underneath his T-shirt. He then filled the box with what few items were left in the desks on the first row of the bunch, reached to peel off Alex's calendar, added it to the box, and exited the room.

As he walked towards the elevators once more, Dr. Kahn exited the one locked room, which Hunter had already learned thanks to his trip to the security room held his examination table.

"After you're done with that," Kahn said, never slowing his stride, "come straight back here."

"Yes sir," Hunter said, ignoring the urge to ask why.

Inside the elevator car, he fidgeted as he figured out what to do. When the bell rang, he stepped out and walked almost hypnotically to the incinerator with the box of junk. He counted each door, noted the number of offices, utility closets, bathrooms, before he reached the incinerator chute.

He emptied the contents, saving the Oakland calendar for last. He gave it a wistful look. "I'll figure out a way to fix this, Alex," he said as he put it down the chute.

In a moment of clarity, he figured out what to do. He went to the far wall, took out his smartphone, and took a picture of the incinerator, making sure to get the door to the men's room in the shot as well.

Going inside the restroom, he saw that it was a simple layout. One urinal, one toilet stall, and the sink. He took a photo of the urinal and stall together. Going inside the stall, he set the phone down on the toilet seat and opened up the lid to the tank. He removed the tape containing the USB drives and pasted it to the inside of the lid. He took a picture of the lid with his phone before closing the lid.

Hunter turned to leave. Before doing so, he paused momentarily, took his phone, and made a few more taps on its screen before sliding the phone in the lower, zippered pocket of his cargo pants. With a deep, long breath, he trotted back to the elevator and went back to the ground floor.

Kahn was waiting by the door to the exam room. "Take off your lab coat and sit on the table," he instructed. His face was stoic, his voice low and steady.

"Uh-alright," Hunter said. Remember, he told himself, you can appear hesitant, but don't refuse at this point. He took off the lab coat and folded it neatly on the exam table. Dr. Kahn went to his array of strange looking devices and took out what at first glance appeared like a penlight with a purple glow stick attached.

"You've had no adverse effects from that injection?" Kahn asked.

"Nope. Like I told you, there was no redness, no pain at the injection site. And it was so long ago..."

"Nothing... Not even in the last several weeks?"

Hunter slowly shook his head. "Nothing."

"That's very interesting," Dr. Kahn said. He pressed a button on his device. The attachment began to glow, the purple light washing around his hand. "Because you should have been experiencing something. A vibration, a small prickling sensation. And it should have been intensifying, the longer it went on."

Kahn passed the device over the area he had given Hunter the injection so long ago. Hunter waited for something to happen. A sound, a flashing… but nothing.

Hunter took a chance, thinking now would be as good a time as any to begin the "interrogate" clause in his scroll. "Why, doctor," he said, with overtly false innocence, "you speak as if there was something more than a vaccine in that shot you gave me."

Kahn switched his device off. "Don't be cute," he said. He didn't raise his voice, but he spoke with a degree of severity Hunter wasn't expecting. "I know you know. Now where did it go?"

Hunter glanced behind Kahn's shoulder. There was another flip clock on the wall, next to the security camera, which was not powered on. The clock read 4:27 PM. Too early for Kai. Hunter continued to stall by withholding a response.

"Answer me!" Kahn slammed his hand on the exam table, which made Hunter jump. He bucked his leg back against the side of the table. He felt the special leather anklet under his denim vibrate in response. It didn't seem if Kahn took it to be anything other than a nervous reaction.

"I wouldn't know," Hunter offered. "Perhaps it dislodged and left my system?"

Kahn scoffed. "Unlikely. Well, I suppose I'll just have to give you another one," he said. He visited the gadget counter again, set down the light device, and picked up a syringe. The sight of it alone caused Hunter to tense.

How long would it take the team across the street to deploy once they got the signal? Did they even get it?

Kahn knelt to one of the many small fridges and opened a door, revealing dozens, if not hundreds, of identical looking glass vials. He stuck the syringe needle in one of them and began to draw out the contents.

"There... there has to be another way," Hunter said, genuinely frightened. He couldn't shake away the fear of the needle, no matter how many times Kai and Calhoun had said it may be necessary to endure.

"Afraid not," said the doctor. "Well... I suppose there is, but I doubt you would like it."

Go on, say more, Hunter thought. Make it a threat. Give me an excuse. But Kahn put the needle down.

"Try me," Hunter prompted.

"I'll make you a deal," Kahn said. "We'll go upstairs straightaway, but only if you promise that you won't try anything cute on the way up. Be a good boy, do as you're told, and you'll make it out of this just fine."

That still wasn't a direct threat. He didn't say he would do anything specific.

"Fine."

Hunter's mind was racing - try to run now? Follow through and let Kahn take him upstairs? He looked at the time again. Just past 4:30, and still at least a half an hour before Kai would be able to venture outside.

They walked to the elevator car, and Kahn pressed the button. Hunter continued to think as they stepped inside and Kahn pressed the button for the top floor. He had to think about this carefully. He could hit the emergency stop and try to escape up the elevator shaft... but that would take time. He could make a break for it as soon as the doors opened, but he didn't know the layout of the top–

Kahn pressed a moist cloth against Hunter's face. It smelled a lot like the handkerchief the doctor had let Hunter wipe his sweat with. But much stronger, and so potent that in one muffled breath, Hunter was knocked unconscious.

With his head feeling dense and swirling with confusion, Hunter's eyes opened on what appeared to be a dimly lit, circular room. He was laying on another exam table, and his neck was sore and hot.

Dr. Kahn appeared over his head, examining him. "Fine. That's just fine. That will work famously."

"My neck? Again," Hunter asked groggily.

"Your arms and wrists just won't cooperate," Kahn said wryly, referring to Hunter's notoriously hard-to-access veins from before. "But time is not on our side tonight, so I have to do what I can to make the experiment work."

"Ex...experiment?" *Go on, admit to it all,* Hunter said to himself.

"Again, you can drop the act," Kahn said, "I know you went behind the curtains against instructions."

Play dumb. "I don't know what you're talking about." He strained to look for a clock.

"I place those curtains in a *very* specific position," Kahn said. "When I came back from getting supplies, I found they'd been disturbed."

"The only one disturbed here is you," Hunter said. "That woman had an alligator's scales, Kahn, what *was* that?"

"The next stage of progress, what else could it be?" Kahn said. He wheeled out a device from a far wall and powered it on. It looked like a sonogram machine. "Temporary animal metamorphosis, I call it. A way for humans to exist in extreme conditions. Say someone is stranded in the desert - why not temporarily change your DNA into that of a snake or another animal adapted for that climate? The snowbound could convert into bears and hibernate until help can arrive. I am developing a *service* to mankind." Hunter saw Kahn pick up a scalpel from a bag of gear.

Suddenly, the few lights that illuminated the room died out. The vibrations of air conditioning and other electronics ground to a halt. The power was out. The only light in the room now came from the sonogram machine, which was evidently battery-powered.

Hunter hoped that had been the crew from The Order making their move. He squinted to look at the screen. It read 6:02 PM. *Go-time.*

"Dratted power," Kahn cursed under his breath.

"What's the scalpel for," Hunter asked.

"Oh, the risk of an unexpected result on this accelerated timeline is quite high," Kahn said. "Instead of the expected result... in this case, the development of hawk-like feathers along the neckline, you could simply develop a mass at the injection site."

Like the giant tumor he saw on Alex, Hunter assumed.

"Generally we let those masses express on their own, but we haven't the time for that. I'll simply have to excise it at once, and then we can try again.

"You're insane," Hunter growled.

"Best not to call names of the person holding the blade," Kahn said. Taking off his spectacles, he sneered over the end of the exam table as and fussed with the sonogram.

That had to be enough of a threat. "Maybe so," Hunter said, "but even an idiot would have remembered to tie his subject down while he was unconscious."

Kahn turned to face Hunter directly. "What?"

Hunter pelted him in the chest with both of his sneakered feet. The doctor doubled over in pain. Hunter rolled off the table, landed on his feet, and bolted for the door. He had to fidget with the lock, giving Kahn a few seconds to gather his wits. As Hunter made his move through the door, Kahn swiped at him with the scalpel.

The blade caught Hunter on the back of the right leg. He seethed with pain as he ran at full pace towards one end of the hallway. With the hall a similar layout as the second and ground floors, he had to assume he was heading for the stairwell.

At least this pain has summoned Kai, Hunter thought. *I hope...*

He could feel his sock becoming soggy with his own blood. Praying the slice hadn't gone through a major artery, he fought through the stinging pain and threw himself down the stairs two at a time, hoping to pick up speed. He passed a giant number 3 on the wall next to the door, which he tried to burst through - but it was locked. He heard the door from the floor above burst open.

Hunter bounded down the next group of stairs. Floor 2 - with the security office. No sooner had the door come into his view, he was knocked down from behind as Kahn tackled him, bashing Hunter's head into the steel door. The weight of the two men crashing inward caused the unlocked door to unlatch, and they fell into the open hallway.

Hunter wrenched and twisted his body about. Kahn had dropped the scalpel at some point, Hunter noticed. But he had a powerful grip on Hunter's legs, leaving his arms free.

With a ferocious shout, Hunter grabbed Kahn by the head and jammed his thumbs in the doctor's eyes. Howling in pain, Kahn released his grip, allowing Hunter to wriggle free. Guided only by the emergency exit lights still gently lighting the hallway, Hunter bolted for the opposite end, where another set of steel double-doors were located.

They were locked. The crash bars didn't budge. Panicked, Hunter looked behind him in time to see Kahn disappear into that floor's designated kitchen area. Perhaps he got disoriented. But never mind - through the security glass of the double doors, Hunter could see through to the other side - another in a myriad of large offices cluttered with boxes and desks. There was an explosion of glass as something barreled through, somersaulting expertly across the floor then hopping to his feet like some super powered acrobat.

Kai!

His partner zoomed to the door. He couldn't open it from his end, either. Kai looked into the glass at Hunter, then yelled, "Look out!"

Hunter instinctively turned around, to see Kahn nose-to-nose, just as Kahn jabbed a large butcher's knife straight into Hunter's belly. Kahn withdrew the knife and tossed it to the floor.

He saw stars as his body convulsed. He could hear Kai making an inhuman, high-pitched roar. Hunter sank to his knees in searing pain, putting his right hand against the wound. Kahn grabbed his left hand and began to pull him like a rag doll across the floor. Hunter's body turned with his feet pointing back toward the double doors.

Hunter watched as Kai began to slam himself against the locked doors. They dented once… twice… three times.

"You've got no way out," Hunter gasped, fighting through the pain.

Kahn either didn't hear him or had plunged so far into insanity that he didn't care. He continued to drag Hunter as they passed the elevator shaft. The lights suddenly flickered back to life, catching them both off guard. Kahn, disoriented, took a step backwards, letting go of Hunter's arm.

Kai succeeded in bashing through the doors, running at a frenetic pace towards Kahn. The doctor spun on his heels. In doing so, he slipped on a pool of Hunter's blood that was rapidly spilling onto the floor. He fell. Kai tackled him and without so much as a beat, gripped Kahn's head and snapped it to one side like it was a twig. The body landed lifelessly and slumped against the wall by the stairwell door.

"Hunter!" Kai scrambled on his hands and knees to his lover's side. "Oh, ye Gods..." He took his wrist-communicator and pressed the button harder than he'd ever pressed it. "Mugan! V-Medic to Level 2. V-Medic to Level 2." He pressed both hands into Hunter's stomach. Blood bubbled through his fingers.

Hunter was struggling for breath already. "Kai... phone... phone..." he murmured.

"Shh. Shh. Save your strength, Hun," Kai said.

Hunter slapped a bloody hand over Kai's as he began to gasp. "Zipper. Phone."

Kai, registering what Hunter was trying to say, reached into Hunter's pants pocket. He pulled out the phone. The screen was still on the video recording app, and the word 'REC' was blinking. The battery had 2% left.

"Evidence," Hunter panted. "Security office. Tapes... Kai, I'm... I'm..."

"No. No. Hunter, no, you're not," Kai said, letting the phone drop to the floor. "I am not losing you. I can't."

Hunter's eyes began to flutter. His breath became shallower.

"I can't," Kai repeated. His fangs began to descend. "I must, but ye Gods, what if I miss again..."

The sound of Order agents beginning to run throughout the hall and past them began to fill Hunter's ears. It was so disorientating.

Hunter knew he only had one breath left, two at most. Staring Kai in the eyes, he took one big gulp of air.

"I trust you, love," he whispered. "Go."
Kai dove for Hunter's exposed throat.

11

DISCIPLINARY ACTION

Hunter gagged as he sucked on the bottle of blood. "I thought you said there was flavored stuff you could use to mix into this stuff," he complained. He took another tug on it and retched.

"You have to get acclimated to how the pure stuff tastes," Kai said. He gave a soft and understanding smile and ruffled Hunter's hair. "You must feed on real blood for at least two weeks before we can start trying out the fun additives."

Hunter groaned, took another couple gulps of the blood, then set the bottle down again. "Can you tell me what happened to Alex and the other patients?"

"You really ought to focus on regaining your strength right now," Kai said. He curled up next to Hunter on their bed and pressed the button on his remote to lift up the shutters.

"I did help in the investigation," Hunter said. "I'd like to know what happened."

"I know, but there's time for all that. Look," Kai said, pointing to the shimmering Dallas skyline. The night was clear, so the stars and the quarter moon were shining brightly in the area outside the city lights.

"Quit changing the subject," Hunter said.

Kai sighed. "Well, we had to bring them down to Dr. Ife's offices so she could work on the antidote to bring their skin back to normal. Then me and some of the other vampire agents had to user our influential powers to wipe from their mind the entire period of their abductions. That took a few days to safely do. Then we figured out where they all lived and crafted situations for their returns."

"How do you mean?"

"Well, to wipe three, four whole weeks of a person's memory, and then to replace it by giving them constant messages about what their cover story is going to be… it can kill brain cells, actually," Kai said. "It has to be done in many short sessions. The guy from Colorado, for instance, is going to have to believe he got lost on a hiking trip and hitchhiked back to his hometown."

"Alex's USB drives - what were they?"

"A program called 'Compile & Condense' that allows terabytes of information to be compressed into a single thumb drive. The other one, once we used Alex's password trick, was the full contents of his work PC," Kai explained, "including a full journal he was keeping about the DRS project. He was actually a volunteer for this whole thing."

"What? A volunteer? That file labeled him as having been selected."

"That was a smokescreen devised by the doctor," Kai said, "after he learned Alex was trying to blow the whistle on him. Alex started out as a willing participant then tried to quit when the experiments started affecting his health."

"Ah," Hunter said. He took another chug from his bottle. "And Alex? Is he gonna be alright after all this?"

Kai frowned. "No, Hun. He's not." He paused to collect his thoughts. He could sense Hunter's stunned reaction thanks to their new blood bond.

"When our agents were loading him up to take him back to HQ," Kai explained, "that... tumor-thing, on his chest... it basically imploded. The toxins went straight into his lungs. He didn't... he didn't make it out of Inner-Core alive, Hun. I'm so sorry."

Hunter sat there in shock. He blinked and opened his mouth, but only a small crackle of sound left his throat.

"We had our friends with the county coroner's office take his body," Kai said, taking one of Hunter's hands. "We explained the situation; they're going to remove the mass, clean him up, locate his nearest family. They're going to declare it meningitis or something bacterial; the evidence will be there to back it up."

"They can do that? Don't they have their own oaths or something?" Hunter was surprised with how incredulous he sounded.

"It helps to have connections in the medical community, just like we do some of the law enforcement we deal with," Kai said. "It wouldn't do his family any good to hear how he really died. At the hands of a mad scientist trying to turn people part-animal?"

"Somehow, it doesn't feel right," Hunter mumbled. "Especially when someone murdered him - what about the justice part of closure?"

Kai sighed, looking back at the cityscape outside their window. "What matters is we got justice for Alex. And the others. And you," he added. "I still feel really guilty for what I did. Greedy and guilty."

"You did it because you love me," Hunter said. It was his turn to grip his partner's hand. "I didn't want to die. And I'm not... technically. If I had to pick someone to go through eternity with, I'd want it to be you."

"Thank you, Hun," Kai said. He kissed Hunter on the lips.

"Thank you, Vampy," Hunter said as he returned the kiss.

Kai wrinkled his nose and chuckled slightly. "Vampy?"

"Possible pet name," Hunter said. "Trying it out. Thoughts?

"We'll talk. We'll see," Kai teased.

There was a buzz from Kai's phone. He tapped the talk button and held the phone to his ear. "Yes. Alright. Send him on."

Kai gave an uncomfortable smile to Hunter as he put down the phone. "More good news on the way," he said sarcastically.

Hunter changed out of one band T-shirt and into another, and replaced his pajama bottoms and sat on the living room sofa. Annabelle purred contentedly in his lap. Across from him sat Kai in one chair, and Calhoun in the other. Calhoun sat somewhat stiffly in his chair with his attaché case across his lap. He tried to smile softly as he spoke.

"You, ah, have a lovely home here," he began.

"Thank you," said Kai, threading his fingers together. "I spent a lot renovating it."

"It shows," Calhoun said. "And, uh, Hunter. I hope you are... improving."

Hunter had been zoning out through the pleasantries. "Oh! Uhhh, yes sir," he said, scratching between Annabelle's ears, causing her to flex her claws happily.

"I should tell you, uh... Hunter, that you are up for an award for your bravery and your... um... being wounded in action."

Hunter blinked in surprise. "Oh. Really. Well, that's... that's very kind of you sir, thank you."

"Oh, it wasn't me, it's our overseers, really." Calhoun didn't mean for that to come off sounding as if he didn't care. He cleared his throat. "So, Agent Taylor, I suppose you know why I am here."

"I reckon I do," Kai said flatly.

"I don't," Hunter said, "but Kai said I might as well sit through it, so... let's hear it?"

"While we understand the circumstances surrounding Hunter's recent... change of status, shall we call it?"

"His vampirism," Kai said, folding his arms across his chest. "That's what it is. He's a vampire now."

"As you say," Calhoun said, opening his case. "There is, unfortunately, a very clear rule about an Agent turning anyone into a vampire in the course of his duty."

"It was a fellow agent," Hunter said.

"And he was on the brink of death," Kai added. His body position was tensing quickly.

"Be that as it may, doing so in the field was extraordinarily dangerous," Calhoun said. "If it were to be done anywhere, it should have been here on your premises or at HQ under the supervision of Dr. Mwodim."

Kai sighed out of frustration. "Fine. Got it. So what?"

"So, there has to be a disciplinary report made," Calhoun said. "Believe me, this isn't what I want to do. I'm being made a frickin' Human Resources secretary here, but the decision from the overseers is this: Agent Taylor, you are hereby suspended for two months, effective tonight."

Kai rolled his eyes. "Fine. Whatever. I suppose there's something for me to sign..."

Calhoun handed Kai a single paper and a pen. Kai scratched his signature into it and handed it right back to his supervisor.

Calhoun rose from his seat. "Again, I didn't want to do this."

"It's fine, sir. I get it." Kai stood up as well. "I don't like it, but I get it."

"I'll see myself out," Calhoun said crossly. "Hunter, please get well soon. You can take all the time you need."

He made a quick exit out the front door.

Kai whipped out his phone. "Security, Calhoun's on his way out; please give him clearance."

"Is it serious?" Hunter coaxed the cat to perch up on his shoulder. Her purring kept his anxiety from creeping up as he asked.

"Yes and no," Kai said. "It'll go in my file. Enough of those infraction notices and I could be terminated."

Hunter gulped. "Which kind of terminated?"

"Both." His expression softened as he saw the worried face of his lover. "Hey, don't worry about it. It's the first one I've ever received, and I've been in this organization quite a long time."

"So let's try to turn a negative into a positive," Hunter decided. "We have two months to do whatever. We could watch lots of movies, we can talk more about your history, mine if we have to," he winked as he said this, "and just relax."

"We can," Kai said, going to the kitchen and taking two bottles of blood from the fridge and zapping them in the microwave. "In between your training sessions."

Hunter groaned.

"Now, listen to me, love," Kai said as the microwave beeped and starting warming their food. "Remember what I said to you; you have a lot to learn about being part of my kind, and a relatively short time to learn it in. It takes much longer to learn how not to be a monster than it takes to get it right."

"Okay," Hunter said, accepting another bottle of blood from Kai and beginning to drink from it. He did find this one to be less bitter and metallic than the one before. "So what is this training going to entail?"

Kai sat down, nursing his own bottle. "I think we'll start tomorrow evening, with a lesson I call 'Movie... and a Dinner.'"

They drove into Arlington the following night for the next-to-last showing of a summer blockbuster at the Studio Movie Grill. As the crowds exited, Hunter and Kai stood in the lobby.

"Movies sure have gotten louder since the last time I saw one in the theater," Kai said.

"Really? What was the last one you saw?"

"I saw *Citizen Kane* when I was in California last."

Hunter cocked his head. *"Citizen Kane?"*

Kai nodded. "Mm. Say what you will about it being a historic piece of cinema - all the stories about Orson Welles being a pompous jerk were right on the money."

"Wait." Hunter turned to face Kai directly. "Are you telling me you were at the *premiere* of *Citizen Kane?*"

"Yeah," Kai said plaintively. "I was part of a team hired to guard the screening room when he watched what was shot each day. He didn't want any gossip about who the film might have been about to be made public before it was completed."

Hunter stood there, nonplussed.

"So let me ask you a question," Kai said, putting his hands in his pockets. "Did you feel alright during the movie?"

Hunter thought about it earnestly for a moment before replying. "About midway I started to feel overwhelmed, a bit."

Kai nodded. "All the nuances in the soundtrack, the sounds of the people in front of us talking, the chewing and crunching from the family to our left...?"

"Yeah!" Hunter ran a hand through his hair. "It was so weird, I could hear virtually everything going on in that auditorium."

"What about smells?" Kai started to walk slowly towards the exit doors. Hunter followed.

"Now that you mention it, yeah," Hunter said. "Besides the popcorn, that's a given in any theatre – but it was like I could smell every dinner item that was being brought in there."

"Think about this, and close your eyes if you need to," Kai instructed. "Five seats to the right of where you sat, and three rows down – what were they eating?"

Hunter balked and stopped. "What? Are you kidding? How could I..." he stopped mid sentence when a thought smashed into him like a punch to the face. "Sirloin steak sandwich, medium-rare, garlic aioli and a side of truffle fries."

"What did he have to drink?" Kai stopped walking and looked at his vampire progeny.

"A Moscow Mule before the show," Hunter said almost immediately. "Two colas with dinner and an Irish coffee during the final act."

Kai nodded. "Those are your heightened senses and situational awareness clicking into high gear," he explained. "You may not be paying attention to them in the moment, but your brain is filing away every sight, every smell, every taste and every texture you encounter. How does it feel?"

Hunter started walking for the exits again, smiling. "A little kickass, I've gotta admit."

Kai smiled. Hunter had noticed the one dimple made in Kai's right cheek the first time he'd seen him smile. And that was when Hunter had been mortal.

"It's easier to do in enclosed spaces," Kai continued, opening the exit door and letting Hunter pass by. "A little harder outdoors, so you may have to concentrate a bit harder."

Hunter nodded. "Heightened senses," he said. "And, judging from present company, super speed and the ability to fly."

"Which we'll get to another day," Kai said. As the theater patrons passed them by, heading to the main parking lot in front of the building, the pair continued walking towards the far end of the building. "Any questions so far?"

"Just one," Hunter offered casually. "Why did we park so far away from the theater?"

"So that we could practice part two, the 'Dinner' portion of the evening." He motioned for Hunter to slow his pace, and they walked casually past strips of stores and restaurants that had closed for the evening. They continued on near the east end of the shopping center, where a new phase of the district was still under construction. A four-story concrete parking garage was complete, but hadn't officially opened. It was where Kai had parked his black sedan.

"Ah, so you figured we were going to be followed by two guys in biker gear?" Hunter asked. They didn't bother turning their heads.

There's three there actually, but one's about to split.

Hunter glanced at Kai, who hadn't spoken aloud. He was smirking with a certain degree of glee.

I think this is one of our best abilities, to be honest. Telepathy. Go on. Try it.

Nodding, Hunter simply thought about what he wanted to say. *Uhhh, let's see um here uh what could we oh ... mmm... testing? Testing? Do you read me?*

Kai snickered out loud. *It's not a CB radio, Hun. Just talk to me. Picture me in your mind having a conversation like we just were.*

Hunter cracked his neck, a habit he developed long ago when he was trying to concentrate on something deeply. *So, you think they're going to follow us to where we parked?*

Kai nodded. *There've been reports of muggings on the edge of the property at night. Mostly drunk people, so if you want to act a little tipsy to 'sell them' on us, feel free.*

Passing an unlit path light, Hunter suddenly grabbed hold of it and pretended to retch. Kai stumbled back a pace or two, pointing and laughing. Hunter righted himself after a moment and the two continued to walk.

You should be able to hear them from this distance, Kai advised. *Give it a try.*

"They look like they're pissed," said one.

"They better have cash on them this time," said the second.

"Whatever they have, get it and let's get the hell outta here," said the third. "I'll meet ya'll back at the gas station; I gotta fill up."

There were sounds of fists bumping. Hunter could hear three distinct pairs of footsteps become two.

Right, Kai transmitted to Hunter. *When we get into the garage, I can make a quick jump to the opposite end from where we parked. What I want you to do is take my keys and pretend you're getting in the driver's seat. They'll make themselves known. Then I'll join the party. Just go with the flow.*

Hunter nodded in confirmation and held out his hand. Kai tossed him his keys as they reached the unlit parking garage. Kai took a few steps ahead, then disappeared from view.

Hunter hummed softly as he walked towards the car. For added effect, he tripped over nothing in particular, took a few hobbled steps, and put the key in the door.

"You know it ain't safe to drink and drive," said a thick Texan voice.

Hunter turned to find the two bikers. One had a bald head and was about a foot taller than his partner, with cropped red hair and a chain dangling from one hand.

"Annnnd what particular business is it of yours?" Hunter slurred.

"Oh, we're the Safety Patrol," said the shorter biker, beginning to twirl the chain around his left side. "And my buddy here's right. You can get hurt *real bad* if you try to get in that car right now."

"And what will make the Safety Patrol get off my *ass* and let me get in my car?" Hunter was having as much fun as he had back in high school drama club.

"Cash," said the taller Texas-brogued biker. "You gotta pay the fee to get outta the garage."

Hunter raised his hands as if to say "I give up," and reached for his wallet. "Wait," he said. "I'm getting confused. Am I paying you to get out of here or are you keeping me from driving off - which is it?"

Looks of genuine confusion crossed the bikers' faces as they pondered the question.

"Shut up!" The shorter one sped up the spinning of his chain. "It's a robbery - give us what you got!"

They advanced towards Hunter, giving Kai just enough space to fly behind them.

"Actually, you've got something *we* want," he growled.

The two muggers spun on their heels to see Kai, his eyes glowing red, his fangs fully extended, mouth open in a hiss.

Something primal and, dare he think it – wicked – boiled within Hunter's body. He got a thrill seeing Kai act like this. He was enjoying the sense of fear and confusion the two thugs were kicking out. And the hunger, the sheer *hunger*, caused his own fangs to grow. As the hunger intensified, Hunter noticed a light in his peripheral vision - a red glow from behind his eyes.

I take the big one, you take the redhead, Hun.

Kai leaped towards the bald lummox. Hunter jumped, surprised at the spring at his step catapulting him towards the smaller thug. The shock of the sudden attack caused the thug to drop his chain, which clattered noisily on the poured concrete. They both fell to the ground, but Hunter maintained a tight grip as he awaited instructions.

Hunter could hear Kai and the bald guy smack against the sedan, causing a warning beep from the sedan's security system.

You'll see the vein in his neck throbbing; that'll be the one to aim for. All you need is one firm bite; his blood pressure will do all the work for you. Stop when I tell you to stop.

Hunter could hear the bigger biker plead and scream as he was bitten. The scream died away quickly as Kai put a hand over his mouth. Hunter did as he was told and looked down at the redhead's neck as he protested and tried to struggle. He saw a large vein pulsating and drove his head to it, biting down and puncturing the vein. His mouth filled almost instantly and he began to gulp the contents.

Four mouthfuls will be enough. Count them out. One... Two...

Three... Four...

Hunter continued to suck down the blood. He was lost in the sheer beauty of the moment. He expected it to taste so awful, but this tasted... transformative. It was full of life, full of experience, full of heat and excitement and fear and–

"HUNTER. AS YOUR MAKER, I COMMAND YOU TO STOP."

Hunter felt a force pushing him off the biker. He blinked as he looked around.

His biker remained laying on the ground. His legs were moving in circles, as if he were trying to run away while still prone. Hunter sat just a foot or two away. He looked towards the sedan. The bald biker was seated, slumped against a concrete support pillar, snoring. Kai stood beside the car, arms folded, staring at Hunter.

"Wh.. what happened?" Hunter asked, rubbing his head, confused.

"You didn't follow instructions," Kai said. "Four long pulls is more than enough food to get us through a whole day, maybe two.

"The fact that you couldn't pull yourself away means you're still susceptible to bloodlust," he continued. "We have to drum that out of you. If you drink for too long, you kill. We do not kill without a direct order; it's the pledge we took."

Hunter nodded and wiped his mouth. Fresh blood smeared across the back of his hand. "And what happened just then? Did you pull me back?"

"The Maker's Command is the only telekinetic power I have," Kai said, "over you or anyone or anything. It uses a lot of energy."

Hunter tried to stand up but was kept in place by a continued force he couldn't control.

"It's a time out, in other words," Kai said. "While I move these guys to that far corner, you just sit there and... think about what you did."

"Did you really just talk to me like a father?"

Kai gave him a glare, a grin, and a wink, then started dragging the bald guy to a corner of the garage still bathed in moonlight. While he crossed Hunter's path to drag the mumbling and emotionally crippled redhead into position, Hunter thought about how much work he had to do in order to adjust. Some things clicked right away; he'd have to really practice other things, like his self-control.

"You're out of the penalty box now," Kai said. "You can stand. We still have to set these guys up for morning."

Hunter accepted Kai's hand as leverage and stood up. They walked to the corner where the thugs were seated, heads against each other. As they walked, Kai explained how to gain a human's influence.

"You lock onto their gaze," he said. "Just like you focused on talking to me telepathically, you focus on sending them a message, but you say it verbally."

"You mean talk," Hunter said. "I talk to them."

Kai sighed. "It's more intense than that, Hun. It's a two-tiered connection. It's the stare that tells them what emotion to hang onto. You hold them with the stare as well as the message. Just follow my lead."

Kai put a hand underneath the bald guy's head and tilted it, causing the man to open his eyes with a flutter. As soon as they did, Kai's eyes began to glow bright green. Hunter remembered him saying this was meant to instill calm in his target.

"Don't worry, you big lug," Kai said. "You just got a little wild at the bar. You and your buddy here thought you parked your bikes in this lot, but you got lost. You're just gonna sleep it off 'til morning."

"Sleep it off til morning." The big biker's voice was monotone and robotic. His head then rolled back to his shoulder, a small trail of drool leaving the corner of his mouth.

Kai's eyes stopped glowing. "Your turn," he said to Kai.

"How do I do.. the green thing?"

"Whatever emotion you want to attach, have it ready in your eyes, add to it with your words," Kai said.

Hunter nodded, and as he reached to pick up the redhead's chin, he thought his own calming thoughts. As the young thug's eyes opened and met Hunter's, he could feel his eyes altering again. A glowing aura of green light surrounded his field of vision, and he knew he was in.

"You're very safe," Hunter intoned. "You just overdid it tonight and got lost. You're going to take a nap here in this garage."

"Nap in the garage..." replied the thug. Hunter relaxed his hand, and the man's head rested softly on his chest. The green light went away from Hunter's eyeline.

"Very good, Hun," said Kai. "Really good."

"Thanks, Vampy," Hunter said with a smile.

"Yeah, still not sure about that. Oh, before we leave, you need to heal the bite marks," Kai said, pointing to the wounds on the redhead's neck. "You can either lick them directly, or lick your thumb and give 'em a quick smear."

Wrinkling his nose a bit, Hunter lifted his thumb and gave it a long lick. He then knelt down and rubbed it against the guy's wounds. As soon as he moved his thumb away, the bite marks began to shrink and seal up like two halves of a sweater being zipped together.

"Wild," Hunter whispered in awe.

Kai patted him on the back and motioned him towards the car.

"So, if I can't call you Vampy, what can I call you," Hunter asked, tossing the keys back to Kai.

"What's wrong with Kai?"

"You call me Hun, but your name's already short. What's it short for?"

They opened their respective doors and climbed into the sedan.

"My given name was Caeden," Kai said. "I think it was rooted in Gaelic or something. In the 1960s, I'd been around a hundred years, I thought I was due for a change, and in researching the hippie and surfer culture I came across the name Kai."

Hunter took out his phone and tapped some buttons.

Kai started the ignition and looked quizzically at his lover.

"Kaidan," Hunter read. "A japanese word. The 'Kai' part means 'mysterious and rare.'"

"That sort of describes me, I guess," Kai reasoned. "What about the other part?"

"When used with 'dan,' it generally refers to ghost stories."

"I'm not a ghost," Kai said, starting to steer the car toward the exit.

"I'll work on it," Hunter sighed.

They shared a laugh as they drove away from the parking garage, leaving their prey asleep to wait for the morning light.

12

LEARNING CURVES

After a lengthy shower, Hunter found himself staring absently into the full-length mirror over the linen closet door. His fingers ran across the middle of his stomach, where there was still the faint hint of a scar where, just about three weeks ago, an eight-inch butcher's knife had catalyzed his transformation into The Order's newest vampire.

"It'll be gone completely in another day or two," Kai said, leaning against the door connecting the bathroom to their bedroom. He walked toward Hunter, stood behind him, and gently kissed his neck. They both gazed at their reflection.

"I thought it would have been gone when you turned me," Hunter mused.

"It was a very nasty wound," Kai said. "Kahn even twisted the handle; it messed up your insides. Even the dose of vampire blood I gave you can only do so much, so fast."

"And the Evermore..."

Kai nodded. "We used up all the supply we had in reserve. And we mixed in extra proteins and minerals. It acted, more or less, like adding putty to a hole in a wall. It helped keep everything... intact during the change.

"You healed up beautifully though, beautiful." Kai kissed Hunter's cheek and embraced him tightly. Hunter returned the kiss to Kai's closest hand.

"You did a lot for me. I'm not sure how I could ever repay you."

"Just... be my partner, from here into the hereafter. That's all I ask," Kai said. "I love you so much."

"I love you too," Hunter whispered. He continued to examine himself in the mirror. "Why don't we... why don't I... look better?"

"What do you mean?"

"Well, I don't claim to have had the best physique when I was alive," Hunter said, "but I would have thought I'd at least have developed a muscle or two. Maybe I'd have dropped a few pounds."

Kai snickered a bit and released his hug. "Vampirism isn't a weight loss plan, Hun. It's not a fitness plan, either. Mainly because there's no such thing as the 'perfect body.' I mean, look at me." He flexed exaggeratedly before the mirror. "You don't see a six-pack on me, either."

"I suppose..."

"I don't know the exact science behind it. But just like with our other senses, our vampirism allows us to take our bodies for what they are and puts them at their fullest potential. And I'm not sure, maybe our advanced brains know how to make our bodies defy what the mortal world understands to be the limits of gravity and physics.

"I can't explain it," Kai said, a twinkle in his eye as he spoke, "But damn it, I love what I can do. I love being able to use my abilities and help people, even if they never know they're being helped. And I love that you get to experience it with me."

Hunter could sense Kai had excitement growing within him as he spoke. "What do you want to do?"

"I want to go for a *run*," Kai said gleefully.

"A run? At midnight?" Hunter scoffed. "You're not trying to track down more robbers for me to feed on, are you?"

"No way," Kai replied. "Something much more exhilarating."

"I don't call this exhilarating," Hunter shouted. "I call it fucking *insane*!"

"What?"

Hunter rolled his eyes and transmitted his thoughts to Kai telepathically. *I think this is crazy. I used to be so afraid of heights!*

Hunter was standing on the top of an 80-foot-tall light pole. So was Kai, his pole directly across from Hunter. Between them were the hundreds of cars driving 70 miles an hour or more in either direction of Interstate 35 South. The highway was bathed in the light from the poles they were standing on, beacons that stretched out for miles.

The wind was swirling around Hunter. Even so, he was able to slowly shift his feet so he could turn in place and see Reunion Tower and the other Dallas skyscrapers, their lights a dazzling array of color and shape. *You can't beat this view, though.*

Hey, Hun – focus, Kai chided. *We're here to continue your training. Face southward again.*

Hunter did as instructed. The view wasn't as impressive, but the taillights veering off toward the horizon was still an interesting sight.

This stretch of road goes on for about 10 or 12 miles before we get to an interchange, Kai thought. *All we gotta do is run from here to there and back again.*

What if I fall?

Focus, and you won't. But if you miss a landing, just float to the ground and hop back on the pole again. Use these things as the starting point on a track. Use them to push off of, get your height going, land, and push on the next one. Here, watch me.

Kai crouched low and sprang high into the sky, arcing perfectly towards the next light. He made three perfect landings, ending about a quarter mile from where Hunter watched. It reminded Hunter of watching a character in the old video games, jumping from platform to platform.

See? Nothing to it. You try.

Hunter steadied his nerves. He crouched in much the same way as Kai had. He put his left foot further behind than the right. He pretended he was on the track back in high school, listening to the coach count the runners down.

Three... two... one... go!

Hunter pushed with his left foot and jumped. In a split second, he watched the highway below him get smaller and smaller, as his leap sent him soaring about a hundred feet higher into the sky.

Whoops. Misjudged that jump... He remembered being on the Slingshot thrill ride on a trip to Florida, and how the wind rushed by him vertically as the ride flung him upward. This was the same feeling, but without any safety harness keeping him in a seat. This meant he needed to focus on the bit where he started to come down.

With laser focus, he saw the next light pole and aimed for it. As he came close to contacting it, he looked ahead at the next fixture ahead of him. When his right foot barely grazed the chrome on the light pole, he pushed with his toes. He began sailing, gliding almost, to the next pole, and so on until he landed on the one directly across the highway from Kai.

That was intense! Hunter communicated.

Shall we finish the course then? Kai offered.

Without responding, and with a playful grin, Hunter leaped from his pole and continued south. The two vampires took it in turns, leapfrogging from light fixture to light fixture, for miles and miles. Just as they passed the Dallas city limit, a tangle of highways and exits appeared, and the pattern of lights changed dramatically.

Stop at this next one, turn around, and we'll head back downtown, Kai transmitted.

Hunter amazed himself at the speed and ease with which he was moving. Untethered, unrestrained, the wind swirling around him, giving way to him, as he jumped and flew from pole to pole. He loved being able to look down in between each launch, seeing the cars below, none of them aware that two human bodies were hurtling themselves on an urban playground of their own making.

The pair eventually sailed past the place they started their relay, deciding to come to a comfortable rest atop the Greyhound station at the edge of the downtown district. From there, they had a decent view of the TV tower, still lit and glowing, near the building secretly home to The Order.

Kai looked at it, a mixture of fondness and sadness washing over him. "I know it's just temporary," he said absently, "but it feels like I've been banished, y'know?"

"I can get that," Hunter said. "It's just for a few more weeks, though."

Kai nodded. "True enough. It's just odd having all this free time."

"Why don't we head back home," suggested Hunter. "We can spend some of that free time building all that flat-pack furniture you said you bought a decade ago, turn that spare room into a home office, once and for all?"

As they arrived home, they saw their two guards at the gate, standing with worried faces. One had a hand clamped on one side of his neck.

"Gray, Duffy," Kai said, exiting the car. "What's going on?"

Both men were in their late 40s and were dressed like cowhands common for the rural area where the compound sat. Hunter could see the shorter one, the one with the hand on his neck, was bleeding. He exited the car as well.

The taller one responded to Kai. "We had a breach, sir."

"What kind of breach, Duffy? Is Gray gonna be okay?"

"I'll be fine, boss," Gray replied. His voice was ragged.

"I went up to the front door after seeing someone run from the porch," Duffy explained. His voice was soft, yet authoritative. "While I looked into what was going on, somethin' attacked Gray here. It had to have been another vamper."

Hunter motioned for Gray to let him examine his wounds. When Gray let his hand go from his neck, Hunter and Kai could see what appeared to be six puncture marks, in what seemed like the pattern of an upper set of teeth. The holes were still oozing slow rivulets of blood. Hunter made a quick trip to the car and pulled out a first-aid kit. He unwrapped a package of gauze and handed it to Gray, who accepted it with a small, embarrassed expression.

"A six-fanger," Kai said. "There haven't been any from that faction in this area for some time. What about the house, is it secure?"

"It is," Duffy replied. "No forced entry, no sign of a break-in, but there is some vandalism to the front door."

"What kind?"

"Spray paint, I think. Some sort of tag. I wouldn't expect a gang or anything of that nature out here."

The tone in Kai's voice alerted Hunter to something very wrong. "No. Not of that nature." Kai looked at Gray, still dressing his wounds. "Hunter, could you, uh, see to that? I need to go look at the door."

Hunter nodded as Kai made his way up the gravel road to the house, jumping over the still-closed gate to do so. He approached Gray, who was still wincing over the pain of the attack and the still-open wounds. Remembering what he'd done in practice, Hunter channeled calm thoughts until he felt the green aura begin in his line of vision, then caught Gray's eyes. "It's going to be fine," Hunter said. "I'm sorry this happened. We'll try to figure out who did it. But you're alright now."

"Alright now," mimicked Gray, softly. Hunter gave his thumb a lick and wiped it across the area of the bite. He had to do it twice, due to the number of teeth marks. But in moments, the wounds healed. Hunter broke his gaze, nodded politely to each guard, then jumped the gate and followed Kai's path to the house.

Kai stopped just shy of the last step up to the porch, staring at the mark left on the door. As Hunter caught up to him, he saw the symbol for himself. It wasn't red spray paint; they could both tell from the scent, it was blood. It looked like the culprit had painted a capital M and a capital W combined, with the prongs of the W elongated and tipped with dots. There were two horizontal lines underneath that. It almost looked like a...

"The Crown," Kai muttered angrily. "I can't believe it. The Crown has resurfaced."

"Hunter, I should like to introduce you to Noah Frank," said Calhoun. "He is a V-Division member and is Head Recordkeeper."

"How do you do," said Hunter politely. Noah was lanky and as skinny as a rail, with thin-rimmed reading glasses sliding slowly down his nose as he offered his hand. They shook hands and Hunter motioned for them both to take a seat.

"Noah, do you want some B-positive? I'm heating a couple of bottles and could chuck in one more," Kai offered.

"Thanks, actually," Noah called over. "I haven't had a chance to feed tonight."

"Water, boss?"

Calhoun cleared his throat. "No thanks," he said. He waited until Kai had made his way to the living area, passed out the food, and sat down beside Hunter, who noticed Kai's body was almost entirely tense. His eyes were even starting to turn hot-coal red. Hunter mentally pleaded with Kai to calm down, and it seemed to work as they clasped hands with each other.

"Agent Reeves," Calhoun began, "this conversation is mostly for your benefit, as Taylor and Frank already know the background. You will need to know the history as you will be the leading point in this investigation."

"Me?"

"You'll need to do most of the legwork for right now, Hun," Kai said. "I'm still in the penalty box. I can't even set foot in Headquarters until my suspension's over."

"The Crown," Calhoun continued, "indeed appears to be reforming. They do this every several decades in a continued and, may I say, delusional attempt to achieve... what would you call it, Taylor?"

"Certainly not world domination," Kai said. "They're too disorganized to ever achieve that."

"Chaos," offered Noah. He had a voice Hunter likened to a big brother. It comforted him the moment he heard it, which, in turn, helped Kai further. "They like to create a sense of unbridled chaos."

"It helps their allies - terrorist groups, mainly - achieve their own goals," Kai explained. "Wherever The Crown operates, there could be worse things planned."

"And they're here," Hunter said.

"With Taylor out of commission, we need you to read up on every file we have on The Crown, their operatives, past and present, and begin the process of shutting them down again and determining who they may be working with," Calhoun said. "They're like roaches. You can fumigate them, chase them out... but they always seem to regroup and appear again."

Noah took off his reading glasses and put them on the coffee table. He met Hunter's gaze. "You'll have full access to my department," Noah said. "If you need help, you'll have me available and my assistants, too."

"You will start first thing tomorrow night," Calhoun said.

"What about you?" Hunter turned to Kai. "Are you in some sort of danger?"

"Hardly," Kai said, waving the question away. "I've dealt with them before. As Calhoun said, they are a thorn in our sides every couple of decades, but we usually get them cornered, confronted, and disbanded without much issue."

Hunter didn't buy it for a second. "Kai, they painted a fucking warning sign in blood on your door."

"It was just their symbol, Hun," Kai said. "A calling card, nothing more. An invitation to play their game once again. It's what they do."

Hunter chewed on one side of his cheek, his foot tapping nervously on the ground. "So I shouldn't worry about you."

"You shouldn't worry about me," Kai repeated.

"I believe that's all we need to discuss for now," said Calhoun. "We will be putting extra men here at the compound -- just standard procedure with incidents like this," he added, noticing Hunter's expression. Hunter did appreciate his boss trying to keep him calm. "Report to Agent Frank's office as soon as the sun's down and begin your work."

They all stood, bid their respective goodbyes, and Calhoun and Noah exited the house, leaving by the front door, a pink, washed-out version of The Crown's symbol still staining the oak.

Kai locked the door behind them, then turned to face Hunter. "I know what you're thinking."

"Were you and Noah together once?"

Kai blinked. "Okay, I didn't know what you were thinking."

"Were you?" Hunter repeated.

Kai paused. "Yes." Hunter tensed. "It was a long time ago, it didn't work out. He and I decided we'd be better as friends, and there's nothing for you to be worried about. Okay?"

Blushing, Hunter sank his head. "I wasn't really worried about that," he said. "I just... I could feel something, in the way he spoke, that just kinda... told me."

Kai sat back down on their sofa, pulling Hunter down to sit beside him. "He does care about me, very much. And I, for him. But that's after several decades of working together as investigators. And I wasn't the same vampire I am with you. I was in a dark place, closed off, combative, almost self-destructive. He helped me break out of all that. And we explored if that meant something deeper between us. It didn't. And that leaves us where we are today."

"There's still so much about your life I don't know about," Hunter said. He took a long drink from his B-positive.

"We have time," Kai said. "I promise, I'll share my whole history with you. I am an open book with you. After all," he added, "we are writing a new chapter together."

RESEARCH & DEVELOPMENT

Kai hadn't been kidding when he warned Hunter about how dark and lonesome the Hall of Records could be. With Noah leading the way, Hunter followed into the elevator that took them further underground than Hunter had yet been at headquarters. They arrived at a fairly long hall, with a marble floor that caused every sound made, particularly hard-soled shoe contact, to echo wildly. The further they walked, the deeper underground they went, and the thunderstorm that had been thrashing the building outside became buried in silence.

"The Dallas office is the home to every scroll ever issued by The Order," Noah said with an air of pride. "Once a mission is completed, no matter where in the world it is, the assigned agent signs off on it and rushes it back to us for filing."

"Impressive," replied Hunter. "How many scrolls are there?"

"Hundreds of thousands," Noah answered. "All meticulously hand-inscribed with a calligraphy pen, rolled and delivered to agents with a red silk ribbon - a ritual that's been -- pardon the pun -- handed down from the very first day The Order was created."

"Which was?" Hunter was genuinely curious.

"October the 11th, 1684," Noah said. He announced the date with reverence - he took considerable pride in his workplace and it showed in how he spoke of its history. "Mr. Calhoun's most distant relative founded the organization."

Hunter gazed upon the gilded portraits lining the hall, fixtures just above each painting the brightest source of light in an otherwise dim corridor. The brass markers underneath each piece of art noted a familial connection with his boss. "And he just leads this branch," Hunter noted, "not the whole thing?"

"There has been a council in charge of the issuance of our missions and directives," Noah said. "Not even Calhoun is privy to the details of their identities. But it's assumed, although never proven, that Calhoun's great-great-great grandmother is among the members. She's the only known member of his family tree to be a vampire."

The portraits ended, replaced by steel doors, a sign on each noting a span of time - about 75-100 years - and a keypad rather than a doorknob. Noah reached the last door, "1950-present," tapped in a seven-digit number on the keypad, and waited a brief moment.

The door opened, revealing a large room with filing cabinets from floor to ceiling, and a large onyx reading table lined with chairs. It looked like a swanky library rather than an office records room.

The table already had several large stacks of thick files. Noah motioned for Hunter to take a seat, which he did. "This should be enough to get you started," Noah said. "Within these files you'll get a feeling for how The Crown has operated since their formation, plus some of their schemes from the past 70 years or so."

Hunter nodded. He put his cell phone on the table next to the stack of files, sat in one of the comfortable but posture-rigid reading chairs and started to work.

What struck him is how identical The Crown seemed in comparison to The Order - just nefarious. The Crown was a global network of spies, agents, and informants, just like The Order. They used technology and supernatural forces to achieve their missions - Hunter paused to consider himself among those "supernatural forces" The Order relied upon before continuing to read further.

"The Crown has been involved in several failed assassination plots," he read to himself, "and they have strong ties to organized crime and global smuggling operations. Their members are incredibly wealthy and influential people from all over the world..."

Hunter stopped reading. He turned to Noah, who was pulling more files and paperwork from various cabinets. "Was Dr. Kahn involved with The Crown?"

"Indeed he was," Noah said. "I'm preparing a file on him now. It's over on my desk if you'd like to review the notes."

Hunter decided to continue reading the files in front of him. They began to describe Kai's history in fighting Crown agents.

For many years, Kai was known as the most formidable opponent to The Crown's plans. He had taken down their agents one by one, foiling their plans and saving countless lives in the process. For this reason, he had become Enemy #1 on their list.

The Order's various branches had helped Kai stay a step ahead of The Crown by providing him with information about their upcoming missions and activities so that he could be prepared to counter them. This arrangement had worked well; while The Order kept Kai safe from harm, they also got the benefit of having an elite agent combating The Crown's nefarious plans on their behalf.

Missions ranged from stealing priceless artifacts from museums or government buildings, to stopping plots for bombings or destruction of important infrastructure, to assassinations of important figures in the political or corporate world who had been discovered to be Crown operatives.

The Crown would "go dark" after the biggest plots were foiled, usually for a period of 5-10 years before The Order would get word of regrouping and possible new activity.

The last major thwarted mission of chaos was noted in the files as happening in 1995, when Kai stopped a plan to unleash a deadly bacteria on the population. The mission's leader, known only as "The Magus," was behind this plan and had acquired the bacteria from an unknown source. He had promised his followers that if they completed their mission, he would give them eternal life.

Kai had obtained a "carte blanche" scroll authorizing him to track down and eliminate The Magus and his followers, which took him across several continents. The sojourn brought him to an abandoned castle in Europe.

After a fierce fight, Kai managed to defeat all of The Magus' followers and finally cornered him at the top of the castle tower. Kai revealed to The Magus that he knew about his ultimate goal - to acquire eternal life for himself - revealing that it was never part of his plan for anyone else. In a fit of rage and desperation, The Magus attacked Kai but was easily defeated. Before Kai drained him of all his blood, The Magus' final words were reported to be "Gibson will have his due."

"So, this Gibson," Hunter asked, "he's The Crown's leader?"

"We think," Noah replied. "There's never been much evidence leading us to the top of The Crown's food chain. For all we know it could be a council of people. It could be a pseudonym used to describe a single person, no matter how many times that person is replaced. It could even be a" –

Noah was interrupted when his cell phone began to buzz frantically. So did Hunter's. They both looked at their screens. "Tornado warning," they both said.

"I'd better call Albert, tell him to batten down the hatches," Noah said. He began *to thumb through his contacts list.*

"Albert?" Hunter began to look through his phone for Kai's number.

"My partner," Noah explained. "He works the day shift here in the Hall of Records. The yin to my yang, you might say; the day to my... well, you know."

Hunter silently nodded as he looked at Kai's name on his phone. He still felt odd knowing that Kai and Noah had once been... together... in all the same ways Kai now was with him. Ignoring the urge to ask Noah more about that time, he dialed Kai's number.

"Hey, Hun," Kai said. "Checking up on me?"

"Yeah," Hunter said, "we just got a tornado warning here at the office."

"My phone went off too," Kai said. "I sent the guards off for the night, it feels like it's gonna get rough."

Hunter tensed. He hated storms. Growing up in Nebraska, and living in North Texas, he'd seen just about all Tornado Alley had to offer. "Should I come home?"

"No, it's getting too stormy for anyone to be out," Kai said. "This place is pretty secure. And as far as security goes, you're in one of the safest spots in the country!"

"Well, alright," Hunter said. "Be safe, I guess, and call me if you need any" –

His phone beeped four or five times in quick succession. The call cut out. Eyeing Noah, he could see his phone call died, too.

Their vampiric ears could pick up the piercing whine of a siren blaring from outside, several floors above them; a tornado must have been sighted nearby.

The dim lights flickered and died quickly, plunging the two into darkness.

"It's okay; give it a second," Noah said. "The backup system should kick on." They waited, but instead of the return of the amber and white lights, a series of red lights powered on. "The failover," Noah said. "There must be a citywide outage."

A loud crash sounded outside and Noah flinched. "We should probably find someplace to sit it out until the power comes back on."

Hunter nodded, thinking. He wanted to ask the question that had been bugging him since he'd seen Kai and Noah together at the house. He looked at Noah tentatively. "What was it like...when you two were together?"

Noah sighed, a soft smile crossing his face for a moment before fading away again as he remembered. "It was an ill-advised experiment, one that ended after only a few weeks. But we remained good friends afterwards. We didn't let it affect our working relationship too much either; The Order has always been a priority for both of us--even if sometimes I think Kai puts it above his own safety."

"Kai said you helped him through a rough patch," Hunter said. "What was that about?"

Noah looked away as the thought carefully about how to explain it. "It was a few decades ago, after the accidental death of Kai's last lover. He told you about that, right?" Hunter nodded. "He was...devastated. It turned him into a different person; combative, aggressive, reckless--all the qualities that make him so effective in the field made him hard to live with outside it. I didn't know what to do; all I knew was that if we didn't get some control over his self-destructive behavior, it would botch an investigation we were working on at the time and more people could die."

Noah shook his head as if remembering something unpleasant. "I went to talk to him about it, and it wasn't easy," Noah said slowly. "He had built up such walls around himself that nothing seemed to reach him anymore; not even my words or our history together. But eventually he softened and began responding to my offer for help. That's why we took the step of trying a deeper relationship. We both made the same mistake in that, believe me. We both realized we didn't have that kind of bond. It's obvious, though, that you do. And I couldn't be happier for it; for him and for you." Noah smiled and Hunter could tell it was genuine.

A loud thud reverberated throughout the room, and the bright red lights were replaced once again by the subdued reading lamps. Hunter and Noah took a relieved sigh in unison - the power had been restored. "We should go back upstairs and see if we're needed," Noah said. "It sounded like we may have taken a hit."

They took a series of stairwells and hallways rather than rely on the convoluted elevator system, just in case the power went out again. They made their way to the main floor. There was no visible damage to the inside; with the office built within the shell of the existing building, they had avoided any direct contact with the tornado.

"We've got about a dozen cars tossed around in the parking lot," Calhoun shouted above the cacophony of concerned workers. "Please remain here until we get confirmation there are no downed power lines or other hazards outside the building!"

A buzz from Hunter's phone led him to check the screen; phone service was back, if not a bit spotty. There was a text from Kai - "Checking the property for damage and then going down the road to check the neighbors are alright. Love you, stay safe."

Noah tapped on Calhoun's shoulder. "Anything we can do, sir?" he asked dutifully. Calhoun gave a brief nod. "Yeah, we've got a few people stranded on the upper floors of the main building. Power's out in their main elevators, and the stairwells are a mess. We need some able-bodied people to help get them down."

"We can do that," Hunter said as he and Noah rushed towards the stairs. As they climbed up the flights of stairs, Hunter couldn't shake off the image of Kai out in the storm. He knew Kai was more than capable of taking care of himself, but he couldn't help but feel a sense of worry gnawing at him.

The inner core, the cinder block structure housing the "secret" compound, ended, and Noah and Hunter found a large door bent in towards them. Peering into the small window, they saw a few people huddled together behind a large desk. The wind was still blowing strong, and the rain was blowing in through a shattered picture window. The cause - a large oak tree had hurtled through the building. A strong branch had landed into the door, causing it to be handily damaged.

"Hey," Noah called out to them, "we're here to help you guys down. Just keep your distance until we get the door removed!"

Hunter and Noah quickly used their vampire strength to dislodge the door. They were able to wrench the tree branch free, allowing them access to the room. The five people inside were relieved, but still shaking from the ordeal. Hunter and Noah wasted no time in helping them navigate the fallen tree and into the stairwell to safety. They used their preternatural speed and agility to help everyone traverse over the debris that littered their path as quickly as possible.

Once they had arrived at safety on a lower floor, Hunter was about to ask if anyone needed medical attention when a piercing sensation overloaded Hunter's senses, causing him to cry out and sink to his knees in pain. "Hunter?!" Noah cut through the line of tornado survivors to come to Hunter's aid. "What is it?"

Through his telekinetic connection to Kai, Hunter felt something entering Kai's body; a liquid. He could feel the paralyzing pain of the substance filling Kai's body, and felt Kai being dragged by one leg from their home. Panic surged through him, and he stumbled back as he tried to make sense of what was happening. "Kai's in trouble! Someone's after him! We have to get help!" He shouted desperately at Noah before running towards the exit.

Noah followed closely behind, not wanting to leave his friend in such a desperate state. As they reached the stairs leading to the false building's entrance, Hunter heard sirens blaring outside. He saw the disarray the tornado had caused - and the throngs of people watching.

"We can't get out this way," Hunter said. "How can we get to the house?"

"We're going to have to get back up on the roof and fly," Noah said. "Have you flown under your own power yet?"

They began to turn back towards the stairwells, heading back up to the damaged floor they had just rescued the trapped bunch. "No," Hunter said. "All I've done is run across lampposts down I-35."

"Okay," Noah said, thinking quickly as they bolted up floors. "You're going to have to hold onto my waist and let me do it."

They made it back to the damaged floor, climbed over the oak tree's remains, and crossed the room to the roof access stairwell.

The roof was deserted. Twisted metal and shards of shingles lay strewn about. The wind was still strong and blown debris could be seen airborne. Rain fell upon them like a wave. Noah put a hand on Hunter's shoulder. "You ready?" Hunter nodded, latching onto the back of Noah's waist. Hunter felt a rush of adrenaline course through his veins as he watched Noah take off into the air, his hands outstretched in front of him. The wind blew through their hair and clothes, but he did not feel any fear as they zoomed around and above the buildings, heading out of the city and towards Kai's house.

Just as they were about to reach Kai's home, Hunter heard sirens in the distance - police had arrived to inspect the damage caused by the tornado. He knew this would mean trouble for them if they were discovered flying under vampire power. Noah quickened their pace and soon enough they were at Kai's house. They peered in through a window to find it empty; there was no sign of Kai inside or out. Frantic now, Hunter fumbled in his pockets for his keys.

"Whoa, step back!" Noah pulled Hunter backwards.

"What?" Hunter was shocked by the sudden jolt.

Noah growled softly. He sniffed the air. "Don't touch the doorknob," he warned, taking a few paces back from the porch. "Another vampire has been here."

"How can you tell?"

"We all have a unique scent," Noah said. "You haven't developed the ability yet, but we can usually tell when a vampire we don't recognize has been about. This one's not familiar to me. He smells... foul."

Hunter tried to sniff the air but couldn't detect something that told him "vampire." He did, however, smell something repellant and metallic. He looked at the porch area and, by the walking cane left by the door, a small puddle.

"Silver," Hunter muttered.

The word triggered Noah's quick return to Hunter's side. "Don't touch it," he warned. "Liquid silver is extremely dangerous to us."

"What's it doing here?" Hunter felt he knew the answer, and his heart sank when Noah confirmed it.

"Liquid silver is the number one item in a vampire hunter's toolkit," he said. "It doesn't kill us... but it can paralyze us and keep us in debilitating pain.

"*Then*," he added, "a hunter can kill us."

TRACES

While Noah stood guard outside the front door, Hunter entered the house, on a hunt for more evidence. He found no windows shattered - the light-tight shutters were all engaged. There was nothing to show Kai had been attacked inside the house.

"Silver," Hunter muttered.Outside the house however, Hunter found a scattering of fresh footprints in the muddy grass that led away from the main entrance. The tracks seemed to have been made by a single person and they were too small to be Kai's.

Hunter followed the tracks, going further away from the house until they disappeared at a spot near the trees surrounding the duck pond. There he noticed strange marks on the trunk of one of them, symbols carved into its surface with a sharp object. It was the haphazard W and M with the points Hunter recognized as belonging to The Crown's agents - whoever had taken Kai had definitely been sent by them.

Noah noticed the glint of glass by the trunk. A vial. He wafted it under his nose and grimaced. "The scent of an evil vampire for sure," he said. "And liquid silver."

"What does an 'evil vampire' smell like?"

"We all have a unique scent," Noah said. "The younger we are, the fresher and nicer the smells. The type of life we lead adds to the olfactory marking, too. Someone who devotes their life to peace may have a sweeter, friendlier type of marking."

"And this one?" Hunter was trying to learn more than he truly wanted to know what this being smelled of.

Noah knelt down and took another whiff of the vial. "This one is different," he said, eyes narrowing. "It's an old scent I haven't smelled in a while - something like a mixture of decay and death. Like an old crypt deep underground. It's an old vampire, but one who has chosen the path of wickedness and evil." He leaned forward to smell again, his nose twitching as if he was trying to decipher some hidden meaning from it. "I can also smell sulfur and ash - this vampire has been connected with dark rituals and black magic."

Hunter stepped back in horror, suddenly feeling ill at ease with the scent lingering in his nostrils. It was as if, now he knew what to smell for, it came at him full force. "Now," Hunter said, "where the hell did he take Kai?"

Noah pocketed the vial. "That's going to be harder to decipher. They picked a stormy night because the heavy rain makes it damn near impossible to track their scent. It blends too easily with the reawakened earth and lively air."

Checking his watch, Noah sucked in his breath. "Dawn's in another hour. We're going to have to bunk at headquarters; this is going to be an all-hands-on-deck mission requiring a round-the-clock staffing. You should pack some things, as we may be out on the road once night falls again."

Crestfallen that he had no answers as to where his lover was, Hunter swallowed down the urge to burst into tears. The two walked back up to the house. They knew that it would be an emotional night for them all.

While Noah spoke on the phone, ordering more security to watch over the house, Hunter stood at the doorframe of his and Kai's closet. Staring from side to side, from Kai's half to his, a myriad of scents entered his nostrils. Beyond the usual 'fresh linen' scent of the detergent, Hunter could smell... personality traits. Kai's side smelled of a combination of dark chocolate, lavender and wildflowers, while Hunter's was composed of furniture polish, starched cotton and books. Kai had been one for the finer things in life, leaving behind a trace of scents that spoke to his character - heroic and kind. It wasn't just the smells themselves but how they blended together as one; a unique aroma that could only be described as Kai.

Hunter took one of Kai's sleeping shirts off its hanger and clutched it between his hands. He sat on the closet floor and buried his head in the fabric, taking in Kai's scent. The smell of Kai was comforting to Hunter, but it also made his heart ache. He missed his lover, and the thought of him being held captive by The Crown's agents made his blood boil. Hunter wanted to rescue Kai so badly that he was willing to risk everything to get him back.

Standing up, Hunter wiped the tears from his face and started packing a bag. He grabbed a few changes of clothes and a few essential items. He also took Kai's sleeping shirt with him. It was a small comfort, but it made him feel like Kai was with him in some way.

Once he was packed, Hunter joined Noah in the living room. Noah had finished his phone call and was now sitting on the couch with a serious expression on his face. "We need to go," he said. "We've got a lead."

Hunter stood up, still holding Kai's shirt. "What kind of lead?" he asked, hope rising in his chest.

"A witness saw a car leaving the area around the time Kai was taken," Noah said. "We've got the license plate number. It's registered to a rental company in the city. I've already called in a favor and had them run the plate."

"C'mon," he said, grabbing Hunter's bag. "Albert is going to meet us at HQ."

The Crisis Room at The Order's headquarters looked like a much more grandiose version of the records room. Another, much longer onyx table took up much of the space. 20 chairs were filled. Calhoun, Hunter, Noah, and Albert sat in the seats nearest a large projector screen. Dr. Ife sat by Noah, furiously tapping on a tablet computer's keyboard. Other agents and assistants chattered amongst themselves before Calhoun took a wooden coaster from the table and knocked it against the marble top to gain attention.

"We have a limited amount of time to figure out a game plan," Calhoun said sternly. "Agent Frank, what's the latest on the rental car?"

Noah stood and addressed the group. "The car was rented under a pseudonym, and using a stolen credit card. We know that the car was driven to Love Field. The car was wiped clean of prints, but Mugan confirmed through smell that Kai and our suspect vampire were inside."

"Do we have the vampire's identity yet?" Calhoun pressed.

"For that I refer to Dr. Mwodim," Noah said. "I believe she has an announcement to make." All eyes turned to the doctor as she rose to her feet and buttoned her lab coat.

"Ladies and gentlemen," she said. "I had planned to release this project at a later date, but given the urgency of the emergency, I felt it was necessary to bring it forward. The Order is spearheading an initiative to compile an upgraded vampire identity database, cross-referenced by an olfactory search algorithm."

The revelation caused a wave of murmurs. Dr. Ife waited patiently until Calhoun decided to use his coaster as a gavel once again.

"I asked Noah to give me the list of unique scents Oh3e was able to remember from the crime scene and I ran it through the beta test of the search engine. I now present to you a list of three potential suspects in the disappearance of Agent Kai Taylor." She turned on the projector, showing surveillance photographs of three men. She described each one to the group.

"Our first suspect is Mikhail Grigori, a vampire who escaped Kai during a mission about 60 years ago. He swore revenge on Kai and anyone he associated with. A rumored member of the Soverignty Collective, the midwest faction of The Crown, his current whereabouts are unknown." The room was deathly silent as everyone processed the information.

Dr. Ife cleared her throat before continuing. "Our second suspect is Eric Armani, a psychic vampire with powerful mind control abilities. He was spotted in an alleyway near Love Field just hours after Kai's disappearance and has been linked to organized crime in the past.”

“We have Mugan checking out that lead,” Noah interjected.

“Lastly,” the doctor read out, “we have Nicholas Dimitrov, another former agent of The Order who went rogue after going dark on a mission in Rome some twenty years ago.”

Noah leaned in to Hunter’s ear and whispered, “He was Kai’s partner after me. He was only with us for about six months; we think he was a Crown sleeper agent but intel has been hard to come by.”

“If he was taken to Love Field, doesn’t that mean he’s being flown somewhere?” Hunter asked.

Albert stood up to speak. Next to Noah, it was a study in contrasts. Noah was thin; Albert was overweight. Noah was tall; Albert was squat. Noah had sandy hair, while Albert had a shock of curly red hair.

“Not necessarily,” Albert said. “Airports have been known to be organized crime rendezvous points because the noise can mask any untoward sounds and there’s so much activity anyone could miss observing a handoff.”

“A handoff?”

Albert nodded. “We think Kai may be transported across state lines, possibly in the trunk of another vehicle.

Hunter’s eyes widened in shock. Noah gave Albert a sharp look as if to chide him for being so blunt.

Hunter tried to send a telepathic message to Kai, hoping that something might help him locate where Kai was and where he was being taken. He stared intently at the carafe of water directly in front of him, thinking that if he focused on something it might boost his signal.

But it was no good. He may as well have been hearing static; there was no message coming back to him. There was however, a sudden searing pain, psychically transmitting itself through Hunter's body. He grimaced and doubled over in pain. A concerned rumble flowed through the room.

"It's happening again," he moaned. "They're shooting him up with silver again!"

"How long has it been since the last injection?" Calhoun queried.

Noah did some quick math in his head. "Judging from the last psychic episode, about four hours. That's about how long the effects of that strength of colloidal silver impact a vampire of Kai's size and age."

Writhing on the floor, Hunter managed to ask, "How long can he survive like that?"

"As long as they don't boost the dose, indefinitely," Albert replied. "Of course, if they don't feed him" –

Noah shushed him.

Made uncomfortable by the sight of Hunter's distress, Calhoun cleared his throat and motioned for Dr. Ife and Noah to move closer. "I'm not quite sure what to do. It's getting close to 10 a.m., and if each injection is going to do this to him..."

"He really does need some sleep," Noah said. "If he's going to be of any use for the search."

Dr. Ife held up a hand. "I can give him some Evermore with a quick-acting sedative," she said. "He'll be out until sundown."

Calhoun nodded firmly. "Very well. Let's get him taken to some private quarters then. I need to get scrolls issued for our three suspects. Noah, I trust you can run lead on that – but get some rest, yourself, yes?"

"Count on it, sir," Noah said dutifully.

The pain fully subsiding, Hunter felt himself being lifted upright by Albert and the doctor. "I'm awfully sorry, Mr. H," he said. His voice was raspy but friendly. "I didn't mean for my words to cause any upset."

"It's... it's okay," Hunter panted. "I'm so tired..." His face was turning whiter by the second. He could see the black veins creeping up his arms. He needed sleep - but Kai! How could he possibly sleep with Kai who knows where?

"Drink this," Dr. Ife said, as if in response, holding a black bottle marked EVERMORE. "It will help keep that fighting spirit alive." She smiled her kindly smile that was starting to bring Hunter much comfort.

He took the liquid down in one long gulp, and he started to say thank you to the doctor before he passed out.

The next time Hunter awoke, it was dusk. Noah had been keeping vigil over him for the past several hours. He filled him in on what had happened while he slept: Mugan had located Eric Armani in the airport sewers and interrogated him. Armani admitted to abducting Kai and handing him off to Mikhail Grigori.

A chill shivered down Hunter's spine. This was great progress. He had dozens more questions, but he knew he needed to allow Noah to finish his update.

"Grigori, to the best of our intelligence, is now headed in the direction of New Mexico with Kai in a refrigerated van. We don't know the reason or the final destination, but the van's obviously to keep them protected from the daylight and the desert heat." Noah sighed and ran a hand through his hair.

Hunter's stomach twisted into knots at this news. He felt as if his heart were being squeezed between two fists of agony every time he thought of Kai out there, so close yet so painfully far away. He thought of all the ways they could be stopped, but despair seemed like an immovable wall standing between them and success.

Noah put a hand on his shoulder. "We will get him back," he said quietly. His words were soft, but adamant; there was no doubt in his voice or his eyes that this would come to pass. "We need to wait another hour for the sun to set far enough out west. But then you and I are heading out. We will find them..."

He also held out a yellowed scroll, bound in dark crimson ribbon. "And we will kill who is responsible for this."

EMERGENCY BROADCAST

Hunter spent the next hour visiting nearly every department within The Order's network of offices under downtown Dallas - starting with Dr. Ife Mwodim's office.

"I am supplying you with three bottles of Evermore," the doctor said, gesturing to the three black bottles being placed in a black backpack by her assistant. "This," she added, holding up a black plastic pouch, "contains nearly every additive and supplement you are likely to need to administer to Kai" –

"If I find him," Hunter noted solemnly.

"Which you will," Dr. Ife said with her trademark kindly smile. "Have faith, my friend. I want you to pay particular attention to this pair of pills here." She pinched her thumb and forefinger over a perforated corner of the pouch. "This is Prussian blue. When dissolved in the Evermore solution it works as a quick-acting anti-toxin to the silver in Kai's system."

Ife's words caused a genuine smile of hope to appear, however softly, on Hunter's lips. "It couldn't be as simple as that, doctor, just... getting him to drink the Evermore mix?"

"No," she said, matter-of-factly. "Kai will have some recovering to do even with the silver removed from his body. Silver, while not instantly fatal at the dosage we believe is being used on him, can still do harm the longer he is exposed to it. That's why you'll find most of these pills, liquids and powders to be things to boost his supernatural defenses and rebuild what might have been lost."

Her assistant placed the pouch in with the bottles of synthetic blood, zipped up the top of the backpack, and handed it to Hunter. He accepted it and slung one strap over his shoulder as Noah escorted him to the research bureau, where he was to learn more about Kai's apparent abductor, Mikhail Grigori.

Albert and the research team were quick to gather the known information on Grigori, but it wasn't much. He had been a vampire for at least a century, and his bloodline was said to be very powerful. His family line was believed to have originated in the Carpathian Mountains of Romania, far from where he now resided in New Mexico. But what they did know was that six decades ago, Grigori had come into possession of a powerful artifact - an obsidian dagger said to be able to contain immense amounts of magical energy, capable of healing or destroying life as desired by its wielder.

Grigori had planned on using this dagger for some unknown dark ritual, but Kai had managed to stop him just in time by imprisoning him with silver chains and locking him away in a secret location. But somehow in the intervening years, it appeared Grigori had broken free and wanted revenge.

"I have two questions," Hunter said. "First - why was there not an order given to kill Grigori back then? I reasoned that if there were signs he would use his knife to hurt others, wouldn't it be justified to take him out?"

"Since there wasn't clear evidence about the ritual he was planning to perform, Kai couldn't proceed with that resolution," Albert said, pulling a copy of the scroll for Noah and Hunter to observe. "Kai must have concluded that keeping him locked away was punishment enough."

"But he wasn't banking on him busting loose," Noah said, folding the copy and putting it in his pocket.

"That leads me to my second question - what happened to the dagger?"

"Kai took it with him," Noah recalled. "The Berlin branch had it melted down."

"More motive for revenge. Now, an observation." Hunter set down the backpack. "Grigori couldn't have gotten free by himself. I assume those silver chains would have debilitated him enough to keep him from any serious escape attempt."

"Did the team find anything pointing us to an accomplice?" Noah asked.

"Nothing solid," said Albert, running his fingers through his red curls, much like Hunter had observed Noah did earlier. "But the running theory is that Grigori may lead us to Gibson, once and for all."

"Gibson? The guy you all suspect heads up The Crown?" Hunter balked. "Why Kai? Why not try to find the council members of The Order?"

"They're just as impossible to track down as Gibson himself," Noah said. "But if there's anyone in this organization with the history and the track record as our go-to agent... it's been Kai, no question."

Albert's eyes met with Hunter's, and the agent could see the continued anguish washing over Hunter. Albert gave Noah a look, and Noah closed his eyes and nodded.

"Hunter, I wanted to say, again, how sorry I am about earlier," Albert said. "I'm about to send Noah out with you, and I worry about his welfare, just as I know you're concerned about Kai's."

"Honestly, there's no need to apologize," Hunter said. "I understand."

Noah clapped Hunter softly on the back. "There's one more stop we need to make," he said. "The armory."

Hunter stared in utter awe at the hundreds upon hundreds of weapons stockpiled across rows and rows of maple shelves. Each one propped up on a metallic stand like a featured book at a library. Gunmetal gleamed under the fluorescent lighting; the smell of gunpowder and gun oil was almost overpowering.

"We're seriously going to go after this vampire with guns?" Hunter clasped his hands behind his back; he'd always been timid and nervous around weapons. "What, are the bullets filled with holy water or something?"

"That might work if we were in the movies," Noah said with a wry grin. He understood Hunter still had a lot to learn about the lore and myths surrounding vampirism. "No, these are your standard 'full metal jacket' style bullets - pure silver, of course - that will explode upon impact with a vampire body.

"We have some ammo that is filled with liquid silver at a much greater concentration than which Kai is being subjected to. If fired at a vampire target correctly it will instantly neutralize them."

"Neutralize."

"Basically, it will make them explode," Noah said. Hunter gulped in response.

Walking through the aisles of shelves like the clearance sale at a grocery store, Noah picked up a few weapons and placed one each into his own backpack as well as Hunter's. "9-mil," he listed. "A mini-crossbow and six silver-laced tips. Filled with as well as lined... You'll notice most of these things are meant to be used at a distance; we want to avoid close contact as much as possible."

"Because I'm so new," Hunter knew the reason why. "I wouldn't stand much of a chance if it came to a contest of strength."

"Right," Noah said. "The greater the space, the greater the chance he might be able to make a mistake."

"Grigori." Hunter phrased the question like a statement.

"Assuming he's all there is to worry about... yeah." Noah pocketed his glasses and strapped on the backpack.

"So, we've got about 30 pounds of stuff in these bags," Hunter said. "Aren't I going to be weighing you down even worse when we fly away from here?"

Noah tried to not let the words smack Hunter like he was sure they would. "You won't be holding onto me this time. You'll be flying under your own power."

The Dallas Bank & Trust Building was the highest structure in the city. Green neon lights lined the edge of the tower, making it glow like a welcoming beacon to visitors near and far. It also meant it would be very easy to see two figures hurtling up the sides, so Noah and Hunter had to be tactful and use the elevators to get up to the top floor.

Their backpacks labeled with the logo of a pest control company allowed them easy access, and they made it, unquestioned, to the top floor, which was filled from top to bottom with television and radio transmission equipment.

Noah shouted to be heard over all the fans and computer parts whirring and buzzing. "There's like 40 sets of antennas that broadcast from the top of this tower."

"Yeah?" Hunter hollered back. "Neato." He was letting his frustration and fear get the better of his demeanor. "Sorry."

"S'ok," Noah replied. "But these antennas are going to broadcast one more thing: You."

Hunter shook his head in confusion.

"We're coming up on Kai's next dose of silver," Noah explained. "When you feel that injection, you're gonna try to communicate with him again. With your mind. These antennas will be able to drive that signal further than you could on your own. If he's alive... he'll hear you. And if we're lucky, you may be able to pick up on something that will help us locate him."

Hunter processed all this information as best he could. It was yet again more details that would boggle his human mind, yet he had to file it away as yet another thing to learn about his evolving, vampiric existence.

"Let's get to the roof," Noah said. He stepped up on a set of sturdy crates to access the hatch leading to the roof. He unlocked it, opened it, and vaulted himself up before holding out an arm for Hunter to grab onto."

While there had been virtually no breeze at ground level, at 72 stories up, there was a strong, cold bluster. Noah's face was illuminated by the city lights below, and Hunter scanned the skyline with awe.

Noah pointed westward. "So, to fly long distances as a vampire, you'll want to take advantage of the jet stream," he said. "Basically, there's this river of air that travels in a single direction at high speeds. It's like taking a highway instead of backroads; you can make your destination faster if you know how to use it."

He traced an imaginary line in the air with his finger to illustrate his point. "As long as you're going in the same direction as it is, all you have to do is line yourself up and ride it out. You'll get where you need to go faster than ever before."

Noah put his arms up, and the wind made his coat billow like a pair of wings. He laughed, a sound that seemed to be carried away in the tumultuous gusts. "Now you try it!"

Hunter followed suit, albeit with a bit less enthusiasm, allowing himself to be swept up by the air currents he felt around him. As he flew around the top of the building, Noah began teaching him other tips and tricks about flying long distances and ways to prevent draining energy too quickly.

"You've got to find your own flow with the air," he said. "Don't fight against it; learn how to use it as an ally." He demonstrated by gliding through an updraft and using it to carry him higher into the sky before slowly descending again under its waning power. Hunter watched carefully and tried it out himself, learning how different winds interacted with each other and how they could turn them into powerful accelerants or brakes.

As Hunter felt he was getting the hang of it, a sudden burst of pain from his abdomen made him crash to the ground by the door leading to the elevator machinery.

"Hunter!" Noah called. "Is it Kai?"

"Yes," Hunter said, the wind knocked out of him. "It's more than the silver this time. I think he's... I think the bastard is beating him up just for sport!" He felt punches connecting to the face, the chest, and lower. Then he felt the familiar searing heat of colloidal silver entering the bloodstream again.

"Quick - before the sensation fades, get up and start communicating!" Noah rushed to Hunter's side and picked him up. Hunter groaned, his fangs extended in anger. He looked up at the towering spire. The antenna.

Kai, sweet Kai, he telepathed, focusing his eyes on the antenna. *You must answer me. Where are you?*

Hunter could swear he was hearing static in response. *Kai? Speak to me! Where are you?*

Hunter began to hear music. Shrouded in static, he heard singing, and faint strains of bass clarinet, harpsichord, and string bass.

Hunter turned to Noah, utterly confused. "Am I supposed to be getting radio signals back?"

Noah appeared just as confounded. "What are you hearing?"

"The Beach Boys," Hunter said. "The fuck am I listening to?"

"This is K-R-T-Z, 99.7 on your F-M dial! Nothin' but the solid gold oldies, 24 hours a day!" A radio.

"KRTZ," Hunter repeated. "Look that up, will you?" Noah whipped out his phone and started searching immediately.

Kai. Listen to me. We are coming to get you. Noah and me. Hold on, do you hear me? Hold. On.

No... stay away. The faintness of Kai's reply scared Hunter to the core. *He'll get you...*

Just hold on, Hunter transmitted. *We're going to save you.*

"Artesia," Noah reported as he got the search results. "Artesia, New Mexico."

The static, the music, Kai's weak thoughts... they all faded to silence.

"So the intel was right. New Mexico was the goal."

"Appears that way," Noah said. "So we've gotta get on the move." In a series of determined stomps, Noah walked to the edge of the building, stepped up onto the marble-lined parapet, and took a few deep breaths. Turning to Hunter he said, "You ready?"

Hunter clenched his jaw. "Let's do it." He followed Noah's stride and stepped up on the parapet. The wind hit him square in the face, causing him to momentarily lose his balance. He was able to see just a few windows of the floor beneath them.

Time stopped as Hunter and Noah leapt off the building, soaring through the air, westward towards New Mexico. They flew together side by side at an incredible speed, their arms and legs catching the wind and propelling them even higher into the sky. Hunter's stomach began to churn from the intensity of their flight and he found himself filled with wild exhilaration. They were on a mission now - a mission to rescue Kai.

For this moment in time, it felt like anything was possible; like they could fly right up to the moon if they wanted to. And within Hunter, a boiling urge grew, an urge to confront who was responsible for Kai's pain, and deliver it back to them a hundred fold.

16

WHAT'S MINE IS YOURS

Dallas became a distant memory as Hunter and Noah continued flying along the jets of wind. Cities gave way to farmland, which gave way to prairie and to rocky outlands.

Hunter had never felt so powerful as he did in that moment, soaring through the sky as a vampire under his own power. He felt electrified, as if his body had once again become reanimated with energy. All of his senses were heightened and he could taste the air on his tongue and feel it flowing over him like a warm embrace. The stars shone brightly overhead, and Hunter felt a connection to them, as if each one was guiding him on this quest to save Kai.

The speed of their flight filled Hunter with urgency; they had no time to waste - every second mattered now. But at the same time, it was almost therapeutic; despite the danger he was flying into, Hunter felt surprisingly calm and focused. He could still feel Kai's pain emanating from somewhere far away, but it didn't distract from his newfound sense of freedom. As Hunter soared through the night sky with Noah beside him, feeling invincible for just a few moments in time, all fear melted away.

The atmosphere became noticeably drier the further west they went. Hunter reckoned they were nearing the border between Texas and New Mexico. But just as he thought to himself they might make it to Artesia before Grigori made his next tortuous attack on Kai, a familiar sensation of a needle's stick entered his psyche. This time it was a stab, right in the heart.

Pain choked Hunter's body and ruined his train of thought. He curled his body in reflex, causing him to lose all momentum with the air. He began to plummet back to Earth. Noah yelped in surprise and pitched his arms in front of him to begin a rapid descent.

Noah's eyes met Hunter's, and in that instant they both knew what had to be done. Noah extended his arms outwards, forming a makeshift wingspan to catch the air. He darted towards Hunter until their hands touched, and suddenly Noah was there before him; stopping him from free-falling. Together they began to float down gracefully towards the ground, like a pair of balsa wood gliders.

They were so close now that Hunter could feel the heat of the desert rising up from below them. The dust made it seem like he was descending into some ancient dreamland as he watched the tiny city lights flicker in the night beneath him. Finally, with one last gust of wind, Hunter was on solid ground again, with Noah standing steady beside him. The rubber soles of their boots just scraped the asphalt of the desolate highway. Looking from side to side for approaching cars, and seeing none, Noah noted the worn metal sign along the shoulder read "Welcome to Lovington, New Mexico."

Pain still coursing through his muscles, Hunter instinctually sat, bow-legged, on the road, right on the double-yellow line separating the highway's lanes. "This is the worst yet," he groaned.

Noah checked his watch. "It's only been three hours," he said. "The pattern so far's been every four. They're getting impatient."

Hunter let out an agonized scream as the psychic pain Kai's body was sending triggered a sense memory fresh in Hunter's brain - the deep, chilling sensation of steel forcing its way through flesh and bone. He tried to communicate this to Noah, but the pain was so intense he could only clutch his belly and roll onto his back.

The sound of an approaching vehicle made Noah grab Hunter and pull themselves into a ditch near the highway sign.

"Why are you carrying on with this," Hunter could sense Kai asking. *"If you want to kill me so badly... just fucking do it!"*

"All in due time," Hunter heard a voice he didn't recognize. The voice Hunter heard was deep and gruff, like gravel being scraped across asphalt. It was eerily calm, but with a sinister undertone that made each syllable reverberate through Hunter's bones. *"Once your betrothed arrives. After all, you both are guilty of crimes against The Crown."*

The mental transmission broke up. Fighting back tears, Hunter communicated the exchange to Noah. They sat in the ditch, watching the occasional car or truck pass by.

"I can see a cafe about a mile up the highway," Noah said. "Let's get there, do a little research, and plan our next steps."

The Moonlite Lounge Cafe was old, like it was stuck in the late 1950s, and not in a charming way. Worn out dated posters were Scotch taped to the walls and an old soda fountain groaned noisily in one corner. The tables were all mismatched, some with cracked Formica surfaces and others covered with stained green linoleum. A thick, acrid scent of old cigarettes was layered with decades of grease and grime that permeated everything around.

"Why did you order coffee?" Noah asked as he made various taps and swipes on his tablet. "You know you can't drink it."

"I wouldn't want to anyway," Hunter said, holding the mug tightly in both hands. "I never liked the taste, but I've always liked the smell. It calms me down. Makes me think of cozy winter cabins, that kinda thing..."

He tried not to let his impatience take over, but he had to speak. "We can't stay too long. Grigori" –

"Grigori said he's waiting on you," Noah said. "I'm trying to figure out why. And why Artesia? That's the part I can't wrap my head around." "Why's easy," Hunter said. "He said we're both guilty of crimes against The Crown." Noah seemed lost. Hunter jogged his memory. "Remember? Dr. Kahn? He was working with them. Kai killed him, but it was because I interfered with his experimentation."

"Of course." Noah rubbed the bridge of his nose. "I'm just trying to piece things together. Artesia? It just seems so random."

"Well, what goes on there? What kind of place is it?" Hunter put a spoon in his coffee, stirring it slowly. The ripples in the liquid distorted the reflection of his face. His eyes were slightly swollen from the strain of crying and holding in the psychic stress of Kai's predicament

Noah tapped his screen a few more times. "Not a heck of a lot," he said. "Relatively small town, about 11,000 people. Sits on the highway we're on now. Their main industry is... sulfur mines." He paused. Hunter watched as Noah reached in his inner jacket pocket and retrieved the vial of liquid silver he found on Kai's property. He sniffed it again. "Sulfur."

"Wait, you said the vampire who used that vial had a personality that smelled of sulfur," Hunter said, processing the development. "Grigori wasn't the one who used it on Kai at the house... but he must have supplied it. That's who you smelled on the vial."

"Grigori must be camped out at or within the sulfur mines," Noah said. "If his scent marking includes hints of sulfur, it would make sense he'd want to surround himself with enough of it to try and avoid detection by other vampires."

"So we head to the sulfur mine," Hunter said. He felt ready to explode out the door of the cafe and hit the highway running.

"Hold up," Noah said. "It's likely, yes. But like I just said, it may be very difficult to track him by scent alone. And it's a mine, Hunter. There could be dozens of passageways and dead-ends. Not to mention hazards... and maybe traps, as well."

"Are we going to have backup?" Hunter rubbed his temples. "There's a ward that covers this area, I assume."

Noah nodded. "Calhoun assured me there would be. He said to assume there would be eyes on us the moment we crossed into New Mexico."

"So that's as much of a safety net as we're going to have," Hunter said. But he sensed further hesitancy on Noah's part. "What is it?"

Noah looked down. "I just... I'm scared, Hunter. I know this mission is necessary, and we can't turn away from it. But I can't help but think of what would happen if something goes wrong... to me, or even all of us. Then Albert would be alone. He's the only family I have left now. Or you and Kai don't make it out..." He looked out the window at the night sky; a faint sprinkle of stars glinted from beyond thick clouds. He thought back to the moment he had kissed Albert goodbye before leaving for this journey, and his heart sank at the thought of never seeing him again.

Hunter set the coffee mug aside, pushing it forward with one hand. "I've already been through death once," Hunter said. "I can't say I care for it much. But... I did sign up for this. Beyond what's going on with Kai, it's obvious The Crown has something really disgusting planned, if it involved Dr. Kahn and his transformative experiments. We have to do what we can to stop them before they try to go about their plan another way."

Noah closed his eyes in silent acceptance. "Alright then," he said. "We're going down the mines."

The two of them exited the cafe silently and set out, taking to the air above the road which led to the sulfur mine, the air cold and crisp. The moon shone above them, lightening up their path and casting eerie shadows everywhere.

Hunter pointed out the Artesia City Limits sign to Noah, and the small orange lights that dotted either side of the road as they flew above. "We're almost there."

The two men exchanged a glance, their expressions a mix of determination and fear. Before long, they were over the mine, its entrance like a gaping maw in the middle of flat terrain. It was dark and menacing, but beyond it lay something far more sinister–the unknown darkness where Grigori was hiding with Kai, in whatever state he had been left in.

"Look, Noah," Hunter said as they landed. "I have to say something. You and Kai had a thing together, and there have been times the last few days where the visual of you two being... together... has threatened to upset me." Noah blanched. "Oh, Hunter. I'm– I'm sorry. It" –

Hunter held up a hand. "I never handled jealousy well, especially when I had no need to be. It hurt all my past relationships. But I see how you are with Albert. I know what you two have is real - just like what I have with Kai is real. I know I have nothing to worry about. And the level of care you've shown me, as a fellow agent, is... I appreciate it. And I appreciate you."

A soft smile replaced the initial expression of worry on Noah's face. "You've only been a vampire a few weeks, and a working agent even less than that. But you're great at being both."

As they walked closer to the mine, they could see its looming presence like a giant beast lurking in the night.

They cautiously landed at the entrance of the mine, and as they passed heavy machinery and equipment, they scanned for any outward signs of Grigori's presence. They could see that it was an unassuming opening with no visible guards or other protective measure. However, upon closer inspection they noticed a few faint glimmers from something hidden within the darkness that hinted at possible hidden traps inside.

Noah and Hunter looked at each other silently as they pocketed a weapon from their packs before entering. They took their first step into the unknown darkness of Grigori's lair, ready for whatever may come their way as they made their way deeper into the depths of mines. Everything seemed eerily quiet, almost too still.

Suddenly Noah heard a faint click and his undead heart skipped a beat. He and Hunter both looked down and noticed a small pressure plate beneath Noah's feet had been triggered, setting off an alarm in the distance.

He stumbled backwards, quickly scanning their surroundings for some kind of escape route while Hunter immediately stepped forward to inspect the trap with a careful eye. After a few moments Hunter spotted a hidden switch on a far wall that could be used to deactivate it, but it was too far away to reach before they were discovered.

Just then the pair heard a great rumbling coming towards them from the direction they had come. The mine was being sealed off - or worse, a portion was collapsing! Without wasting another second to see which scenario was true, Noah grabbed Hunter by the arm and dragged him towards one of the side passages in an attempt to get away from a shower of stone and rock.

They ran through the narrow corridors, ducking and weaving between chambers of ancient machinery, and eventually stumbled into a large cavern. In the center of the room was Kai's body, laid across an upended mine cart, almost like a sacrifice upon an altar. Hunter quickly ran to his side while Noah scanned their surroundings for any sign of Grigori or his minions.

But just as Hunter was about to reach Kai's body, he felt himself being pulled from behind and yanked away from him by an invisible force. Facing the sky, Hunter felt his backpack full of supplies slip from his shoulders and land with an audible thud on the stone floor.

The telekinetic force gripped Hunter by the throat. He had no choice but to look up near the top of the cavern. Grigori stood tall and proud on the ledge above them, his dark cloak flowing in the breeze like smoke and his piercing eyes glowing with an unearthly light. His grin was cruel and sinister, full of power and malice.

A loud laugh echoed throughout the cavern. "Ahhh, my poor little Hunter has finally come to me! I hope you enjoyed your journey here, because now it ends... with me!" And with that he leapt down from the ledge, grabbing Hunter in mid-air and taking him captive in his grasp.

As he was pulled closer for Grigori to observe him, Hunter stared at the older vampire. Decades of captivity without blood to feed on had taken their toll; it made Grigori's skin gray and leathery, his veins solidified and protruding. His deranged smile showed off yellowed and crooked teeth, including a distinct upper row of six fangs.

"You fed on my security guard," Hunter began to speak, but was interrupted when Grigori placed a hand over his mouth. His fingers were slender and bony, like tiny claws as they clamped down on Hunter's mouth. His hand was like iron, his grip stiflingly tight and unmovable. The skin was rough and calloused from years of exertion, almost like that of an animal.

Hunter could feel Grigori's grip tighten as he spoke, an icy chill coursing through his face. "Silence, you so-called *agent*," he hissed. "Your pathetic maker down there kept me from the blood for 60 years, and interrupted decades of progress for The Crown's planned evolution.

"But I was finally freed two years ago," Grigori's voice became more thick and oily as his vitriol grew. "We were making up for lost time with that scientist. And then *you* and that meddlesome lover of yours came back into my life and *ruined everything again!*" Grigori roared, and with his tight vampiric grip, hurled Hunter's body forward.

Hunter had no time to react and save himself. But he could see two things as he sailed across the cavern: Noah, concealed from Grigori's view in a side passage, loading one of his guns; and the body of Kai, laying motionless on the mine cart... and his eyes beginning to open.

The sight of Kai awakening gave Hunter a split second of hope, but in the next split second, Hunter's body made contact with the cavern wall. He felt bones snap and contort with the impact, and he tumbled to the ground like a rag doll.

Grigori sailed to the ground, standing between Kai and Hunter, laying several yards away. Hunter turned his neck, feeling fragments of bone clicking as he did so.

"So glad you're rejoining us, Agent Taylor," Grigori said, giddily. "You're just in time to watch your lover die."

Hunter could see the silver was still impeding Kai's ability to move under his own power. Grigori could sense it too. He used his telekinetic power to move Kai's head for him, pointing him in view of Hunter's broken body. Kai's eyes were filled with anguish and dread.

Where are you, Noah, Hunter thought. Get this guy, quick!

"And you can also bear witness to the failure of your mission," Grigori said with glee. "I was still able to complete my goal. Bear witness to... evolution!"

Hunter tried to will his body to scramble, but his injuries were severe. Even with accelerated healing, there hadn't been enough time for his bones to reform to the point where he could rise. All he - and Kai - could do was watch as something grew underneath the rear of Grigori's cloak: something that was growing larger by the second.

The weight of this object finally caused it to pop out from under the garment... A giant, reddish-brown scorpion tail, curving behind Grigori's body, elongating and flexing, and preparing to strike.

17

THE TALENT SHOW

Grigori's mouth widened to a deranged degree as Hunter stared agape at the sight of the scorpion-tail stinger twitching above them all.

"Isn't it beautiful?" He flexed the tail again. "The dagger your lover stole from me would have given me this power ages ago. But with it taken from me and destroyed..." Grigori sneered in Kai's direction. He made the stinger of his tail squirt a shot of venom, which splattered on Kai's torso. The shirt Kai was wearing began to discolor and wither. "... I had to let science take its course to achieve the same results."

"You're disgusting," Hunter sneered. He decided his best course of action was to stall as long as possible when he saw Noah emerge from his hiding spot, a gun in each hand, creeping to the back wall of the immense cavern. Hunter also felt his bones latching back into place, like pieces of metal being attracted to a magnet. He just needed a minute or two more.

Grigori growled and stepped closer to Hunter. "You've got quite the mouth on you for someone in your position," he observed. The scorpion tail whipped around, and the stinger scraped Hunter across the face. The venom on its tip seared his skin as it dripped into the wound. It felt like acid. Hunter muffled his scream by clamping his mouth shut.

"I want you to know... killing Agent Taylor here was going to be satisfaction in itself," Grigori said, apparently still unaware Noah was in the cavern, let alone position-ing himself directly behind him from the back wall. "But when I learned he'd sired a baby vampire, and not only that, one he *loves*" - he said the word with sickly-sweet sarcasm - "oh, what joy that gave me. What pleasure I will take from him watching me kill you first..."

Grigori reached under his cloak, and for a brief mo-ment, Hunter thought he was reaching for a weapon, perhaps a silver-filled syringe. But instead, Grigori re-vealed a 1980s-era AM/FM radio clipped to his belt. He flicked it on.

"I've got a brand new pair of roller skates," the cheery female singer blared through the speaker. *"You've got a brand-new key..."* Grigori began to shuffle in the spot he stood, dancing to the music.

The dude is completely insane, Hunter concluded. But while Grigori indulged in the oldies station, it just bought a few precious seconds. He tested his right leg. It was still a bit weak, but he was confident he could stand on it. His arms were fully functional. He began to push himself up with his hands.

As he did, he noticed Noah was in position to take his shot. The moment Noah pulled the trigger, a stream of silver bullets shot from his gun. Hunter instinctively raised his arms to shield himself, but he needn't have bothered - every single one of them hit their mark.

Grigori was struck in several places as the bullets tore through his body. At least one sailed easily through his right shoulder, causing a spurt of black matter to exit his body. The impact caused him to drop to the ground with an agonizing scream. His tail retreated back under his cloak. The distraction was long enough for Noah to race around the wall of the cavern; in a circular, sweeping motion, he flew behind Gregori, picking up Hunter's lost backpack in one arm and Kai in the other.

Hunter pushed himself up and took a few labored but functional steps towards Grigori's body. The scorpion tail was gone. But no sooner had Hunter registered that the older vampire wasn't dead, he saw Grigori's arms begin to transform.

The gray, leathery skin began to turn jet black and scaly, a repeating diamond pattern developing in white scales. The arms began to stretch across the gap between the two vampires, Grigori's hands turning into twin boa constrictor heads. The snakes twirled their way around Hunter's body, instantaneously beginning a vice grip.

Safe from Grigori's view, Noah landed in the passage-way, gingerly setting Kai's prone body upright against the wall. He rushed to unzip Hunter's backpack to view the contents. One of the three bottles of Evermore had shat-tered upon impact with the ground, leaving a blood-red mess over everything. The other two seemed to have survived intact. He grabbed one of the black bottles and opened the cap. Fumbling around, he searched for the sachet of additives.

"Prussian blue," he muttered to himself. "Come on, which one are you... aha!" He caught Kai's gaze - a glazed-over expression similar to someone coming out from heavy surgery. "It's okay, Caeden," Noah whispered softly, using Kai's former name. "We're gonna fix you up."

He took the capsule of blue powder and cracked it open, pouring the contents into the bottle. Placing his thumb over the spout, he shook it up vigorously then put the bottle to Kai's mouth and began to tilt it back.

"Drink it all," Noah said, looking over the rest of Hunter's backpack contents. "But don't be surprised if it makes you feel a bit nauseous. Dr. Ife said the Prussian blue will act like..."

Kai's stomach began to convulse and he stopped drinking. Noah quickly guided him to his right side as he began to vomit. "... like ipecac," Noah finished. Kai heaved and heaved. Noah could see pools of silver liquid shimmering from what was splattering to the ground.

"Atta boy," Noah said, patting Kai on the shoulder. "Finish up the bottle. I may need you in a few moments."

Grigori pulled Hunter closer using his snake-arms. "Pathetic children," he growled. "Do you think this is a game? We're beyond your little guns with their silver-tipped bullets."

Hunter tried to force his arms outward, but the snakes gripped even tighter. His anger started to over-take his senses, and he felt a heat rise around his head. A red glow began to emanate from his eyes. Snarling, his fangs descended and he dove his neck towards the nearest snake body. He ripped his mouth across it like he was eating off a corn cob.

The snake's body burst in a fountain of black goo. The attack was effective enough to make the other snake retract, leaving Grigori with his two regular-size arms once again. Hunter floated himself down to the ground just as Grigori took a flying leap towards him.

They grappled and wrestled, all the while, the elder's oldies radio station continued blaring jaunty tunes about bicycles and convertibles. That ended, however, when Hunter made a ferocious kick to Grigori's chest, the force of which sent him careening into a wall.

A low rumbling began to fill the room, and the ground began to vibrate. Was it an earthquake? Hunter's eyes darted towards the passageway; he saw Noah running towards the opening - and Kai! Standing! But before they could reach the cavern, a large portion of the top dome came crashing down, blocking the passageway and filling the open area in acrid, yellow sulfur dust.

Noah and Kai shielded their faces when the crumbling stone and sulfur poured inward. It had been like an avalanche of snow had consumed the only available door.

"No!" Kai cried, weakly. He ran towards the pile of debris, but he was still too debilitated to do more than paw pitifully at the pile.

Noah coughed and tried to take a deep breath. He shook off the weight of the rock and looked at Kai. "We'll get out of here," he said, determinedly. "We'll get you both out of here. I promise."

Kai shook his head, but Noah grabbed his arm and pulled him forward anyway, towards the pile of rubble that had once been an open door. They both began to dig furiously with their hands, trying to move aside the boulder-sized slabs of sharpened stone, yet when one was removed two more would take its place. Even after caked in dirt and dust they could feel their palms rip apart from the force exerted upon them as they struggled to create even a tiny opening in the wreckage. But it seemed like it was all for naught; no matter how much effort they applied nothing seemed to shift or budge.

Hunter could see through the swirling dust that Grigori had been stunned but was regaining his composure once again. The frustration and fury of it all was becoming insurmountable.

His eyes, which had been glowing red, suddenly stopped when Grigori met his gaze. Hunter's eyes widened, and without any further warning, a new burst of light - purple light - radiated from him.

He had seen auras of different colors from Kai and other vampires thus far - red, yellow, green, blue... but he had never seen purple before. The foreign nature of this one made him nervous.

It clearly filled Grigori with fear. "What is this...?" he asked.

As Hunter bore into Grigori with his sight, he felt a buzzing sensation from within him. It seemed as if his brain was telling him information about Grigori that he shouldn't know.

"What was it like," Hunter said, his tone cold and vicious, "living off of those rats and cockroaches for so long?"

"What?" Grigori paled.

Hunter felt his vision of the cavern disappearing, turning to pitch black. He saw Grigori with 100% clarity, but their surroundings were gone. It was as if they were standing in a void.

"Food was so scarce for you," Hunter said. "Locked away in that dungeon, chained to the ground like an animal. In fact, the rodents and insects who found their way into that room were almost like friends to you - the only friends you'd ever had."

Grigori looked around, from side to side. It was clear that Hunter wasn't just imagining this black void surrounding them... Grigori could see it too. And they both saw Grigori's memories manifesting themselves as Hunter spoke.

"Those poor rats," Hunter said, tapping into his innermost cruelty. He may not be able to hurt Grigori physically, but now he understood how to make him suffer emotionally. "You would play with them, even talk to them. But then the hunger got so bad, so intense... and you couldn't stop yourself..."

They both turned to see the physical representation of Grigori, imprisoned, chained against a stone wall. Weakened by the strong silver bindings and years of increasing insanity, coaxing a curious rat into coming within his reach, before grabbing it and rending into it in a mess of blood and flesh.

Grigori couldn't take the sight, and he curled into a ball, shielding his eyes. But Hunter didn't show mercy; he leaned down and whispered in Grigori's ear.

"You were the worst possible version of yourself," he said. "Killing to survive, no matter how much it hurt you on the inside... wondering what it would take for it all to just end."

"Enough!" Grigori yelled, and with another burst of fury, he barreled into Hunter, knocking them both into the ground for another bout of fist fighting and wrestling. The vision of his encampment dissipated, as did the purple aura around Hunter's eyes.

"Yes, enough," boomed another male voice from high above them. Startled, Grigori looked up towards the broken ceiling of the cavern. Hunter followed his gaze. There was a figure standing just at the edge, staring below at them. He seemed young, almost the same age as Hunter, with long, straight hair that stopped just at his shoulders. He was smartly dressed, in a dark blue suit with white undershirt. He stood with one leg leisurely crossed over the other.

"I'm becoming bored with your display," he said.

"But... but I'm so close to killing him," Grigori protested.

"No, you're becoming weepy and overemotional," the man retorted. He uncrossed his legs and leaped from the cavern top and glided down to the ground where Grigori and Hunter stood. "Quite frankly," the man added, "your little costume drama of turning into animals is becoming less and less like a viable idea -- I mean, think of the costs involved in developing this technology all over again."

"But that's *his* fault," Grigori hissed at Hunter.

Hunter just stood there, unsure of what was transpiring.

"Be that as it may, I fear that this idea of genetically changing my agents may be too cumbersome to realistically implement. I'm afraid I'm terminating our agreement."

"No!" Gregori shouted. "I won't have it! I won't have it! I" -- he made a run towards the smartly-dressed man.

In the blink of an eye, the man held out his right pointer finger and pushed it effortlessly in Grigori's direction. Hunter noted that it began to grow a razor-sharp nail tip. Before he could process what was happening, Grigori had already impaled himself on what was essentially a stake. His mouth twisted in horror a brief moment before his entire body burst, a mass of black and dark blue liquid splashing to the floor like a bucket of hastily-tossed water.

The stranger reached into his suit and pulled out a silk handkerchief, and wiped the stains off his finger. Hunter was frozen in wonder as well as horror.

"Allow me into introduce myself to you," he said with a polite head bow. "My name is Gibson."

Noah strained to hear through the mess of dirt, soot, rock and sulfur. He put the side of his head against the pile.

"What's going on?" Kai said, panting from exertion. He was kneeling against the passageway wall, drinking from the last bottle of Evermore.

"It sounds like there's somebody else in there now," Noah said. "I don't recognize the voice."

"Can you smell them?"

Noah pushed himself off the wall of debris. He was caked in yellow dust. "All I smell is this godforsaken sulfur," he said.

"Hunter, please be alright," Kai wished aloud.

"Gibson, as in... The Crown's... Gibson?" Hunter was astonished.

"The very same." Gibson was admittedly a very striking figure, Hunter said, a thought that admittedly filled him with shame. But it was the man's very presence, his attitude, his sheer confidence, that filled the room with a very different energy.

"Grigori was working for you," Hunter said. "Why did you just... kill him like that?"

Gibson straightened his suit nonchalantly as he replied. "As I'm sure you noticed, the vampire was unstable. And I'm sure his condition wasn't helped by that little... show you just put on."

Hunter's voice caught in his throat. "You saw that?"

The grin Gibson made was at the same time deliberately sexy and vaguely threatening. "Oh, indeed I did. That was a very interesting trick. You simply must tell me how you did it."

Hunter began to back away, and Gibson immediately made a slow and deliberate pace towards him. "I... I honestly don't know how that happened. It sort of just... happened."

A curious look spread across Gibson's face. His eyes moved up and down Hunter's body. "I can tell when a vampire lies to me," he said, matter-of-factly. "You..." he was analyzing something in his head... "are not. Thank you for being truthful with me."

Hunter backed into a wall. Gibson suavely put both hands on the wall, effectively cornering Hunter in.

"You are a bit of a puzzle," Gibson said. "I've never seen a vampire do what you just did, and I've been around hundreds and hundreds of years."

Hunter blinked. What was it he had done? He couldn't explain it even if he tried.

"The former vampire Grigori was trying to make vampire kind evolve through force. Through science." Gibson sighed vapidly, staring at Hunter with a dreamy sort of expression. "It was a nice thought, but you, Mr. Reeves... you have something *natural* hiding within you. It's probably best if you aren't dispatched quite so soon."

He traced a line up Hunter's neck with a finger. Hunter recoiled, in part from the unwanted touch, in part because that finger had just been inside and killed another vampire. "H-how did you know my name?"

"I have a research department too, silly boy," Gibson said. "We know everything about your lover, which, by extension, means we know everything about you.

"Except..." he tapped the corner near his right eye. "That *thing* I just witnessed. It intrigues me so."

Hunter took the opportunity of Gibson retracting his arm to make the gesture and slipped to the side. "There's nothing stopping me from killing you right now," he said.

Gibson made a "tsk" sound with his teeth. "Oh, you know you can't do that," he cooed. "I know the rules of your organization. You can't do me in without one of those little scrolls your people parade around with. And even if you had one, you couldn't possibly do it alone." Hunter had the sense that Gibson was telling the truth about that.

There was a sudden echoing pounding sound from above, past the point where the cavern's top had broken free. They both looked upward but couldn't see anyone.

"I believe you have people coming to free you," Gibson said. He advanced toward Hunter again.

"What are you going to do to me?" Hunter gulped.

"Oh, there are things I want to do to you," Gibson said with a coy smile. He leaned in suggestively until he was just barely touching Hunter's nose with his own. He even descended his fangs as if he was going to go in for a bite. Hunter noticed a distinctive smell coming from Gibson's body. It was conflicting - essences of death and roses, of rotted wood and a fine cologne. "But they will have to wait for another day. Besides, your other half sounds as if he's mending up on the other side of that pile. It's best if I don't interrupt the impending reunion. I'm a sucker for happy endings," he added with a wink.

Gibson spun on his perfectly-tailored dress shoes and made a simple hop up the 40-foot-plus reach to the cavern top, and bounded away down an unseen corridor, leaving Hunter in a state of shock, confusion, conflicted sensations and panic.

The pounding sounds gave way to a cracking sound and the excited voices of four different people in black balaclavas and catsuits. At the same moment, the cave-in debris was knocked through, and out of the rubble climbed Noah and Kai, covered head-to-toe in sulfur dust.

"Kai!" Hunter cried. Kai's eyes lit up and he opened his arms wide as Hunter ran to him. They embraced, tears streaming down their faces as they reunited after what seemed like an eternity apart. Hunter's face was full of emotion, his eyes radiating with love and relief as he thanked the universe that they had both been reunited safely.

Noah looked at the five-foot wide splatter mark of black and blue fluid on the ground. "What happened here?"

Hunter broke the hug. "Grigori was terminated."

"Oh? I'll fill out the scroll. 'Terminated by Agent Reeves,'" Noah said, reaching for a pen.

"Uh-uh," Hunter corrected. "Terminated by vampire Gibson of The Crown."

Kai stiffened. Noah stared in surprise.

"You're sure of that," Kai said fragilely.

"Oh yeah," Hunter said with a forced laugh. "Very sure."

One of the people in all black ran up to Kai and Hunter. "Agent Crispin, V-Division, Ward 6," she said. "Is everyone alright?"

"Taylor is going to need full medical observation," Noah said. "Acute silver poisoning and bodily trauma. Hunter, what about you?"

Hunter shrugged. "Um, I broke some bones, about... thirty of them, I guess. But I'm alright now, I think."

Kai smiled softly. "Give him a look-over, at least."

Crispin nodded. "We only have about half an hour before sunrise," she said. "We need to get you all out of here ASAP."

The trio of vampires exited the mine one by one, each flanked by a Ward 6 agent, into a waiting black van, its windows completely tinted out. Hunter noted the chill of the New Mexico morning air, and the purple sky indicating the dawn of a new day. It struck him how close the purple reminded him of that strange light that enveloped his eyes before...

He still couldn't quite describe what took over him when he confronted Grigori, or how he knew what that scene with the rats looked like. Or why it brought Gibson enough interest to keep him alive.

Hunter knew he would have to tell Kai about it. But not today. He wanted to make the happy ending last as long as he could.

18

LIFE AFTER DEATH

The two months after the Grigori case had been hectic. First there was Kai's recuperation, which took a week - about as long as Hunter took when he was nearly killed and made vampire. Hunter stayed in the underground medical ward in the New Mexico field office by Kai's side the whole time. When Kai was finally strong enough to go back to Texas, he did so hanging on to Hunter's back, who flew them the entire way under his own power.

Noah and Albert, who had been house-sitting and looking after the cat, welcomed them back warmly. "We made a group dinner," Noah said.

They piled inside and made a beeline to the dining room, where there had been laid out three bowls of bright red blood, served soup style, with a tureen in the middle. The fourth place setting held a beautifully-designed chef salad, which Albert sat down to.

"You're human," Hunter breathed, which made the other men laugh. "Yes," Albert chortled. "You were rather preoccupied when we met, I didn't expect you to notice!"

Over dinner that night, they took turns telling each other their personal histories, more for Hunter's benefit than anyone else's. As Hunter looked from Kai, who winked at him lovingly, and from Noah, who gave him a smile of respect, and to Albert, who had the expression of someone who was genuinely happy to make a new friend, Hunter felt at peace with his new life and the bizarre and otherworldly changes that had taken place over the course of nearly a year.

"I do have some news for you two," Noah said. He excused himself and returned a moment later with what looked like a scroll. Instead of being yellowed, aged paper, however, the material looked black. Replacing a crimson ribbon tying the document together was one made of silver satin. He handed it in one fluid sweep to Kai, whose mouth dropped open.

"Fancy," Hunter noted, trying to add levity to a room that had suddenly intensified in tone. A beat passed with utter silence. "What is it?"

"You can't be serious," Kai said, stunned.

"Nope," Noah grinned. "Go on then, open it. Read it all out." Kai pushed his bowl forward and undid the ribbon. The scroll sprung open, and he flattened it across the table, reading the words written in white calligraphy aloud:

"The Benevolent Order of International Investigations does hereby decree and bestow upon Agent Caeden 'Kai' Taylor full tenure within this organization, and the promotion to rank of Chief Investigator for the whole of Wards 6, 8, and 12."

Kai lifted his head and stared at Hunter, who couldn't tell if his lover was thrilled or frightened. "What does that mean?" Kai just blinked in response.

"It means," Noah said, "that your maker here has just been named supervisor in charge of every single investigation happening from here to the west coast of the United States."

"Whoa," Kai finally managed to say.

"Hey, I think that's my line," Hunter said, a smile plastered across his face. He jumped from his seat and crossed the dining room to pick Kai out of his chair, stand him up, and kiss him deeply on the mouth. "That is fantastic news. Congratulations."

"Hold the applause though," Noah said. Clearing his throat playfully, he picked up the scroll and continued to read. "Furthermore, it is hereby decreed and bestowed that Agent Hunter Reeves is promoted to the rank of Chief Recordkeeper for Wards 6, 8, and 12."

Hunter shook his head. "Wait," he sputtered, looking at Noah. "Is-isn't that your job?"

"I accepted Calhoun's offer to take over as Chief Interrogator for the ward," Noah said. "This is all contingent on you guys accepting, by the way. You still have the right to refuse."

Kai and Hunter glanced at each other, already knowing what the answer would be. "We accept," Kai said with a sly smile as he kissed Hunter on the cheek. "Let's do this."

The whole table cheered in approval, and suddenly Hunter felt swept away by all the energy that was radiating around him. He had faced some of his biggest fears over the past year, but now he realized that despite those issues, he and Kai had been able to build something far more powerful than any foe they faced. They had created a bond of trust and respect that made their accomplishments even more special.

As their friends settled down, Noah passed the scroll to Hunter and Kai ceremoniously. "Sign here," he instructed them with a knowing nod before turning back to his own dinner conversation with Albert. Hunter looked around slowly at everyone's smiling faces before taking up a pen from an old inkwell perched near the table's edge and signing his name with a flourish.

The weeks that followed were spent in intensive training for both vampires. They were sent to separate locations - Kai to Barcelona, Hunter to Toronto, to learn the intricacies of their new responsibilities from the best of their international counterparts.

When they returned, there was an official promotion ceremony at the Dallas office. Calhoun presented Kai with a lapel pin. It was shaped like a shield and bore the insignia of The Order - a crescent moon, two stars, and a sun symbolizing the duty of global protection. Inscribed around the rim were the words 'Dedication - Duty - Order.' Under the point of the shield was an additional symbol, the letter V for the V-Division.

Hunter received a gold pocket watch, with the same symbols from Kai's pin and the words 'Time - Organization - Service' engraved on the front. The back featured the same V symbol. They both accepted their gifts graciously, as Calhoun acknowledged their hard work and sacrifices over the past year. He praised them for their dedication to the organization and its mission, thanking them for their commitment to justice and order across all borders. The entire room clapped in appreciation for their bravery and perseverance, culminating in a standing ovation for what they had accomplished together.

Kai and Hunter stood side by side in celebration of this momentous occasion, holding hands throughout the ceremony. As they embraced one another gratefully under the applause of everyone present, they knew deep down that this was only the beginning of something greater yet to come.

Snow was just starting to fall as Hunter woke up. The sun had been down for an hour, but somehow, the chill in the air willed him to stay in bed just a bit longer.

Kai peeked into the room, holding two steaming mugs of blood, which they sipped slowly while looking out the window. "This was a wonderful idea, Hun," Kai said. "What made you think of Colorado Springs?"

"I visited here once, in the spring, with my high school band," Hunter said. "It was nice and all, but I really wanted to see what the place was like in the late fall or winter, when it was nice and cold. And without all the noisy kids cooped up on a bus."

"Well, we have plenty of time to continue enjoying it," Kai said. "We still have four whole weeks of vacation.

They had spent the first two nights in Colorado taking in shows, nightclubs, and just walking together. In the early morning hours the next three days, when the human world had closed up for the night, they explored the mountains and wildlife, even flying into national parks, Pikes Peak, and the Royal Gorge after closing time, a private audience to the beauty of the world.

On this night, they had decided to stay in, maybe take in some time in the hot tub on their vacation home's outer deck. But for now, they were content to stay in the bedroom, watching the snow fall gently to earth. "I know we promised no shop talk during our time off," Hunter began. Kai cocked an eyebrow and waited for Hunter to continue. "But something's been nagging at me. About Gibson."

"About why we're not putting out a scroll for his head?"

"Why?" Hunter couldn't say he was eager to see Gibson dead. Their meeting, however brief, however unsettling, had intrigued him about as much as Gibson had said Hunter intrigued him.

"It's fairly simple," Kai said, climbing into bed beside Hunter. "In all the interrogations I've ever done related to The Crown, those we've terminated have admitted killing or harming people on their own terms - they never implicated Gibson. They never said he gave them orders to act as they did... it was always their responsibility to complete their missions as they saw fit. He only wanted an end result."

Hunter nodded. "And without that clear connection, no orders to terminate." Kai nodded in reply.

Hunter stared at the pattern on the bedspread. Why did he feel a sense of relief at knowing Gibson would remain alive, so long as he took no offensive action? "I suppose one could argue it's a more interesting world with him in it," he murmured.

"Hm?" Kai hadn't heard him but noticed Hunter's pensive look. "What are you thinking about?"

Hunter sighed as he figured out how to phrase his admission. "Something happened in the cavern when I was sealed off with Gibson and Grigori." He explained about the purple aura and the virtual scene he was able to project, which the two other vampires were able to see clearly.

Taken aback, Kai asked Hunter to describe minute details about the dungeon he pictured Grigori chained up on. "That's impossible," Kai said in utter surprise. "That is exactly how it was."

"I was able to read his mind," Hunter said, "like, instantly. My brain picked up on his single worst memory. His biggest fear was being back in that cell. And I was able to... create that world, simply from his own memory. And we all saw it. Is that... is that a thing we can do?"

Kai shook his head. "Nothing I have ever witnessed in all my years," he replied.

"Should I have said something about this earlier?"

"I don't know, Hun. This is... uncharted territory for me. A purple aura, you said?" Hunter nodded. "Have you done this since then?" Hunter shook his head.

Kai bit the inside of his cheek as he thought. "We're going to treat this as a fluke, for now. Before we worry anyone or cause a fuss with The Order. They'll want to experiment on you for weeks and... let's just keep that on hold for as long as we can."

"Alright then," Hunter said. "Are you mad at me? For not saying something to you sooner?"

Kai shook his head no. "Of course not." He rolled off of his side of the bed. "I'm going to go get the hot tub set up. Do you want the outdoor heater on as well?"

"Yes, please," Hunter said. "You sure we don't need to worry about this?"

Kai gave him an unconvincing smile. "Sure, I'm sure."

Hunter nodded and gave a small smile back. "I'll be there soon, Warrior."

Kai looked at him quizzically. "I think of you as my warrior," Hunter said. "I think that's going to be my pet name for you."

"Warrior," Kai said with a smirk. "I could make do with that." And with a small air-kiss, Kai left the room.

Hunter rolled his neck from side to side and decided to brush his teeth before joining Kai at the hot tub. He stopped at the dresser and changed into a pair of blue swim trunks before going to the bathroom.

As he swished and swirled toothpaste around his teeth - and fangs - with the brush, he turned to look outside the bedroom window once more.

It was a breathtaking and picturesque sight: snow-capped mountains in the distance, the twinkling lights of Colorado Springs leading up to the street before him. And, underneath an amber streetlight, staring directly at him, a man with long hair and a cherry-red, tailor-made suit.

Gibson.

Hunter's eyes widened. He froze, toothbrush still in hand, still stuck in mouth.

Gibson gave him a slow, friendly wave and a seductive-looking smile. Raising his hand and pointing to his lips, he mouthed the words, "I. Heard. You." And with a playful wink, he spun on his Italian leather dress shoes and blasted away, leaving a fresh tossing of new-laid snow behind in his wake.

Had that damn vampire really tracked them down just to spy on them and taunt him? Hunter spat into the sink and hurriedly rinsed out his mouth.

And why-oh, why-did Hunter, in the pit of his stomach, enjoy the surprise?

As he burst out onto the back porch, Hunter looked from one end to the other, out against the trees and snowdrifts beginning to build in the valley behind the house.

"Looking for something?" Kai asked, sitting contentedly in the swirling water, steam escaping wildly around him.

Hunter took a deep breath and regained his composure. "Just taking in Colorado's natural splendor," he said before climbing into the tub and sitting by Kai's side.

It's about the only natural thing left in my life, Hunter thought ruefully. As Kai planted a kiss on his cheek, he revised his thought. *Well, besides the love I feel for my warrior, that is.*

END

www.ingramcontent.com/pod-product-compliance
Lightning Source LLC
Chambersburg PA
CBHW051521150726
47997CB00001B/338